An **Uncertain** Faith

Allie Potts

Order this book online at www.trafford.com
or email orders@trafford.com

Most Trafford titles are also available at major online book retailers.

Printed in the United States of America.

ISBN: 978-1-4907-1688-6 (sc)
ISBN: 978-1-4907-1689-3 (hc)
ISBN: 978-1-4907-1687-9 (e)

Library of Congress Control Number: 2013918304

Trafford rev. 10/09/2013

www.trafford.com

North America & international
toll-free: 1 888 232 4444 (USA & Canada)
fax: 812 355 4082

To Ajax, who was with me in spirit every day

Acknowledgments

"Thanks" do not even begin to adequately address the gratitude I have felt during this process for the support of my husband, who always inspires me to make an impact, my family who had to keep up with several draft changes, and moral support from a slew of friends. Without their experiences to lean on, much of this story could not have been told. While this work and the characters contained within are completely fictitious, I would like the record to show that the character known as Charlotte's mom, in particular, is in no way, shape, or form a reflection of my own mother. She would like the public to know that she is much quicker to forgive and willing to see the best in others.

I would also like to extend my thanks to the team at Trafford Publishing for their help in making what had always been a dream of mine a reality.

Finally, I would like to thank my boys, Alex and Liam. You've given me the best causes to laugh at the honest truth, cheer for the small accomplishments, love unconditionally, and reason to curse the toy manufacturers who skimp on including off switches.

Chapter 1

Women's Lib? Oh, I'm afraid it doesn't interest me one bit. I've been so liberated it hurts.

—Lucille Ball

A solitary large tree stood with its branches extending into the recently darkened sky. The air was just beginning to lighten from the day's oppressive heat and humidity, and the leaves and grass all around had just begun to take on that sheen of dewy condensation. The second wave of starlight had just begun to make its presence known as the final blush of red from the sunset left the sky. Beneath the tree, a young couple stood in a loose embrace, neither speaking; the song of the crickets beginning their chirp and the gentle flutter of fireflies taking flight was conversation enough. The man looked lovingly upon the woman, reaching out to caress her face. Her head, as if it had a will of its own, filled the space of his hand as she leaned toward him, eagerly awaiting his next touch that would undoubtedly be a kiss. The woman's body began to tingle in welcome and wanton anticipation, her heart rate increasing as his lips parted. He leaned closer and shouted, "Are you happy with your job? Wouldn't you like to have a career in the exciting world of IT? We can help!"

Charlotte's bleary eyes opened as her husband's arm lifted and slammed down upon the deserving alarm clock. She had t-minus sixty seconds to respond—or less, in the case of today, as the bedroom doors flew open and Jake, her entirely too-awake four-year-old, sprang into the room.

"Mom! Mom! It's waking time! Are you awake? I have to go pee-pee!" He danced around holding himself in support of this announcement.

Her husband of eight years flipped from his side to his back with one arm covering his eyes, the other arm gesturing wildly in the general direction of both their son's noise and his bathroom.

"Then go, Jake! Go!"

Charlotte, more than a little frustrated from the abrupt ending to what could have been a very satisfying dream, wishfully thought back on the days before potty training, but after infancy, as she had no nostalgia about those long nights. At least then Jake would still be confined to his crib until they were ready to collect him.

As rapidly as he arrived, the boy scampered off down the hallway. Their morning routine played out the same way most days, a seemingly unbreakable cycle of wake, redirect, wash, and repeat. With the wake and redirect portion of the program complete, Charlotte arose to start her own morning preparations. She was not the natural risk taker in their relationship, but if she was a gambler, she would have bet that once again Jake had neglected to flush the toilet.

Her husband, Mr. All In, hit the snooze button and, in seconds, was emitting the rhythmic sounds of blissful sleep. With Jake around, there was little risk that he would continue to sleep through another round of the alarm, and so Charlotte left him where he lay.

Though much of the childproofing around the house had come down, occasionally there were pieces still in place, one such being the plastic white-and-gray knob cover that was the only barrier between Charlotte's serenity chamber and the chaos of being the only female in a house full of boys. If she could, Charlotte would spend a blissful hour surrounded by the steam and nothing but her thoughts, but it was another Thursday, which meant another fun-filled day at the office. At least it was that much closer to the weekend. Bowing to the inevitable, Charlotte left the shower so that her husband could begin his own routine while she attempted to detangle and dry her mass of hair.

The fog covered the bathroom mirror. She turned the blow-dryer on it, and the misted surface cleared like a faerie ring, bringing her gray-green eyes contained within a rounded face into focus. Her skin was still marred with a few blemishes and rosy areas even as she entered the latter portion of her midthirties, and she made a mental note to pick up some more skin care products not designed for the teen the next time she was in the cosmetic aisle. She would not attempt to convince herself into thinking she could pass as a professional model, but she liked to believe that even at her age, with a little work, she could still turn the occasional head.

Her hair was once again choosing to be stubborn and rebelled against styling. With every snarled brush stroke, she thought of how nice it might be if she were to cut it all off one day, but Fletcher had always liked it long. She had occasionally chopped it off just under her ears as way of testing the waters, and in each case, the millisecond look of disappointment that crossed Fletcher's face before he regained control of his features told her that, once again, he was not ready for her to make that drastic of a change to her appearance.

Once detangled and dry, her chocolate-colored hair would hit the middle of her shoulders in a glossy wave and look spectacular for the two minutes it would take to finish prepping, before leaving the safety of her bedroom and entering the every-changing shape of chaos that was Jake's room. This morning, it no longer appeared to be a lion's den—last week's passion—but instead stuffed animals and blocks adorned every flat surface with his comforter scrunched together along the floor. Jake announced as she entered the room that the blocks were pirate ships and the blanket the ocean. His stuffed animals were various crew members; Jake, of course, was the captain.

"Ahoy, mateys!"

"Argh, Jake. Would ye be interested in getting dressed for the day?"

"Oh, is it a school day?"

"Yes, Jake, it is a school day."

"Awww coconuts!"

Though perfectly capable of dressing himself, Charlotte enjoyed picking out Jake's outfits for the day if only to ensure that the child that left her house was presentable. Jake was feeling more independent that morning, throwing back the collection of clothes Charlotte brought and picking out his own set.

"I am sorry, kiddo, but you just can't wear that green striped shirt with those plaid pants."

"The shirt is green. The pants are green. They match!" Jake stated this, very sure of himself, as if Charlotte was the one who was fashion blind.

"Honey, how about this one instead?"

"What color is Daddy wearing?"

"I don't know. Daddy, what color are you wearing?"

From across the hall, a muffled voice answered, "Black."

Troubled by this response and knowing how the rest of the conversation will go, Charlotte advised Jake, "He's wearing black."

"Okay, I want a black shirt."

"You don't have a black shirt."

"I want to match Daddy!"

Charlotte sighed. "How about the Mickey Mouse shirt? It has black on it."

"I guess."

Minor crisis averted once again, Charlotte walked with Jake back toward his bathroom to help with tooth brushing and general grooming. As expected, not only was Charlotte greeted by an unflushed toilet; she was greeted by an unflushed and clogged toilet. All the remaining paper had been removed from the roll and was in one shape or form now one with the bowl.

"Jake, what happened here?"

"I needed a telescope for my pirate ship."

With eyes closed and shoulders open to heaven, Charlotte mentally debated if it was worth the pain of being five minutes late to work versus having the mess to clean up when she got home, ultimately deciding to suffer the glare of her boss as she broke up the mess into manageable bits. Fletcher, as he walked by, asked, "Oh, if you are cleaning up the bathrooms, can you get ours done too?"

Three flush cycles and one-half full trash can later, Charlotte joined the breakfast preparations in progress. Fletcher had put himself through school working a variety of restaurant positions and could cook like a chef when the mood and time permitted. Jake regularly showed his appreciation of his dad's skills by demanding cold cereal day in and day out. Charlotte and Fletcher had started out with the best of intentions when their son first transitioned to table foods by only purchasing organic and wholesome cereals. It had only taken one sleepover at Jake's cousin's house for Jake to emphatically decide that if it wasn't brightly colored with a carton on the box, he wasn't interested.

The coffee grinder whirled as Fletcher brought plates of fruit and toast for the adults to the table while Charlotte poured a small bowl of no-brand rainbow corn puffs with a cup of milk. Charlotte had no sooner sat down than Jake put his finger with a large green blob on it on her face announcing, "Mom, I have a booger!"

After hands were washed and noses cleaned, Charlotte and Jake returned to the breakfast table. Fletcher was nearly done with his meal already and busy typing away on his cell phone. Jake, no longer interested in his own soggy cereal, reached over to snatch Charlotte's apple slice, remembering his manners long enough just in time to say please as the fruit entered his mouth.

Without looking away from his phone, Fletcher casually said, "Oh, I need you to take Jake to day care today. I've got a meeting at eight downtown." Charlotte and Fletcher had determined that the best division of labor with regard to the transportation of their son was for Fletcher to drop off and Charlotte to pick up. Fletcher operated his own business, and the belief was that he would have more flexibility in the morning; however, he had begun scheduling more and more 8:00 a.m. meetings at destinations around town, and Charlotte found herself increasingly pulling double duty. It wouldn't be a big deal if she was given advance notice; she would just start her own morning routine a few minutes earlier.

Unfortunately though, the over-the-breakfast status update was more of the norm. Charlotte mentally adjusted her estimated arrival time at her own place of employment by an additional fifteen minutes. She could already hear the sound of annoyance with undercurrent of resignation in her boss's voice.

As Charlotte snapped the last buckle of Jake's car seat, with her hair tasting the humidity in the air and working itself into the usual brown frizz, Fletcher waved them both goodbye. "Don't forget, I have basketball tonight with Tom." Charlotte had.

Fletcher was approximately a foot taller than Charlotte, with a frame that required regular physical upkeep. He had taken up basketball recently with his friend Tom, who just so happened to be married to Charlotte's friend Marie, as a way to burn off the extra calories a person in sales tends to take in from business lunches and extended travel without the payments required of a gym membership. He would return covered in sweat, his normally strawberry blond hair darkened from the moisture, his skin reddened from the exertion, but looking relaxed and happy. Charlotte liked to believe that at least for a moment, she caught a glimpse of the man she had met so many years before. If it wasn't for the fact that she rarely felt she spent any time with her husband, and was left parenting alone night after night, she might actually encourage them. As it stood, a part of her couldn't help being resentful that her husband couldn't somehow fit them into the regular workday. "What's the benefit of being the boss if you can't set your own hours?" she had grumbled to herself on a number of nights.

The basketball games, however, had yet to fall into a regular schedule, often getting cancelled or moved around depending on Fletcher's needs; and Fletcher had begun to complain about muscle soreness and a dull ache in his joints the following day. Even with this reminder in the morning, it was no guarantee that the game would take place later, but it was near certainty that Charlotte would be responsible for dinner that evening, an event that usually wasn't in the best interest of anyone's taste buds.

After being stuck behind a car with out-of-town plates, obviously lost, and Jake successfully dropped off at day care, Charlotte entered her office building. She had managed to regain five minutes by catching the magical light cycle. On the typical drive to the office, there was a string of ten traffic lights; if the cosmos aligned and you hit just the right speed, you could go through at least eight of them without stopping. But more often than not, the congestion on the roadway prevented anyone from achieving the appropriate speed, resulting in stop and go between each signal. School had recently let out, and Charlotte was always amazed by what a difference the lack of high school drivers made to her daily commute. Unfortunately even with the significantly lower volume, Charlotte still found herself stuck behind a pace car with no clear passing option. She sighed as she inched forward. It was going to be one of those days.

Charlotte parked the car and rushed into the office; there was still the possibility that she could be at her desk with her computer fired up before her boss made his mental tally of who was and who wasn't there promptly. He referred to it as management by walking, but Charlotte really just saw it as an excuse for him to criticize those who came in late while he took a leisurely stroll with a hot cup of coffee. As she entered the building, the heel of her shoe snagged on the carpet, the abrupt stop causing her to nearly twist her ankle. She attempted to find a way to save herself from looking like she had just learned to walk, but failed miserably. Her hair decided it too needed a walk on the wild side, as several locks came tumbling free of her updo.

Charlotte worked as a researcher in the patent law office of Whitman and Starnes. Her boss, Richard Starnes, a regular participant in client phone calls, predominately managed the staff and more of the day-to-day operations while his partner took on more of the courtroom litigation and client-facing role. Though she had been with the firm straight out of college, she still did not know whether or not the division of labor had been intentional when the firm was first created or if the two had naturally fallen into those roles. Richard was a heavyset man—falling on the smaller size—with brown eyes, large pores, thinning gray hair, and a handlebar mustache. He claimed that his handlebar mustache was part of the firm's marketing strategy as it made him, and their office by association, more memorable. As if the mustache alone didn't make him memorable enough, Richard also sported a pocket watch on a chain, a relic of that brief period where swing music and zoot suits had briefly come back into fashion in the early 2000s.

Charlotte definitely had not taken the job originally with dreams of making it her career, but the economy had tanked just as she was graduating, and she really was just happy to have a position that could pay the bills. When the great recession occurred and Fletcher lost his job, it became even more important that she continue with a stable, benefit-providing position. As boring as the subject matter was, Charlotte had found that she had a natural gift for the work, enjoying the chance to connect seemingly unrelated cases, tracing patterns and precedents, and writing recommendations. More often than not, she was the first person in the firm to make the connections between cases and had grown accustomed to words of ridicule or disbelief from Richard during the initial discovery until she cornered him long enough to fully explain the big picture. While the regular song and dance between Richard and herself was wearing at times, she had been proven right by the courts often enough to build up a tolerance. Her boss's other quirks were occasionally just as tedious, but she had grown accustomed long enough to them to ignore them most days as well.

Having never gone to law school, Charlotte was well aware that she had reached the pinnacle of her career options within the firm, but unless she could somehow fit in additional schooling around raising her son and supporting the family financially while her husband established his own business, her career plateau would be a necessary sacrifice. If Charlotte was honest with herself, she wasn't sure if continuing in the field of patent law was really something she would be interested in even if neither time nor money was a factor.

Charlotte was brought back to reality by the tune of her computer's welcome sequence followed by the sound of files being dropped into her inbox. Richard hovered over her desk, coffee in hand. "So glad you were able to join us this morning. I was beginning to be concerned that you caught the bug going around. I have a call scheduled in five minutes in my office, and I need you to take notes." "His assistant must be one of those out sick," thought Charlotte. "I guess I am going to work a few jobs today."

Pad and pen in hand, Charlotte rapidly took notes as Richard and the client discussed whether or not their newest product was patentable. Though the person on the other side of the phone was an established client, Richard took delight in instructing them on the basics of how patents operated.

"Take for example a bucket. The first person who created the bucket could have filed a patent claiming that this was a water transportation device and claimed the characteristics within the bucket—stating it is a cylindrical vessel, open on one side, sealed on the other, hollow on the inside, with a component that arcs above the rim, and that this component allows the device to be picked up and transported from one place to another. Now say that someone creates a device that is spherical with two ear-shaped bars affixed to two opposite sides. One could argue that this new device, while also able to carry water, is different enough as the method that it performs this action is in no way in conflict with the established patented design. Therefore, both devices are accepted in the market, except that the patented bucket had a higher cost in product development due to the patent filing and subsequent failed litigation. Patents are only as good as they are defendable."

Charlotte gradually tuned the balance of the client conversation out. She could recite that bit of instruction verbatim at this point, and due to the similarity in the types of conversations that occurred in this office, Charlotte had the ability to continue writing what she heard while on autopilot without actually listening to what was said. Richard was always happy to throw out his bucket example with clients as it was an additional five minutes of billing. Charlotte's pen continued writing until the phone was returned to its cradle. "I'll need those notes typed up and filed by 10:00 a.m., Charlotte." Setting unnecessary due dates and times along with overuse of first names were just a couple more of the reasons a line of potential employees weren't drowning the office in applications.

First task of the morning accomplished, Charlotte returned to her desk to review the stack of paperwork that had seemingly quadruplicated during the short call. Ironically, even though exposed daily to the newest advances in technology and invention, the office still relied on hard copy paperwork, which gave Charlotte the welcome excuse to walk over to the coffee machine; however, she was waylaid along the way by the frantic wave coming from Matt Richardson, a newly degreed young associate intern who was staring at a nonfunctioning copy machine like an archeologist considering whether or not to open a newly discovered prehistoric tomb. Matt was sharp as the serious cheddar he was eventually going to make in his career, but a complete mess when it came to office technology. No one at the office minded his particular handicap because it allowed several of the other ladies on staff a chance to help him in his time of need.

Matt in no way, shape, or form looked like he belonged buried under stacks of manila file folders and paper shredder dust clouds. He had a youthful face and chiseled body that deserved to be out in the public's eye and puppy dog eyes that just begged for attention. Charlotte knew that several of the other ladies found him to be outright gorgeous, and numerous discussions had taken place in the ladies' washroom about the various forms of personal training they would give him if he but asked.

While Charlotte considered Matt to be far too young to suit her personal tastes, she had to be honest with herself that looking at him occasionally made her job a fraction more bearable. If the looks weren't enough, Matt was a hopeless romantic. Hopeless in the regard that while the good looks attracted a number of dates, he was still holding out for his unknown soul mate. Charlotte and several of the other ladies were frequently asked to offer their advice as to how to let yet another girl down in a way that wouldn't leave permanent emotional scars.

"It's jammed again, and I can't figure out how to fix it. I've pulled knob A and lever B, but I can't find access tray C, and honestly, I don't know why I need to as I've already pulled out the actual paper that was stuck. But it won't restart until I finish this sequence."

Charlotte pulled out the offending tray and completed the balance of the eight-part sequence. The whirl, rattle, rattle, drum told them that the copier was back online and ready for its next job.

"You are amazing, Charlotte! I don't know what I will do without you!" Another crisis diverted, Charlotte picked up her coffee and started to return to her desk and the stack of paperwork that would most likely be at least two file folders higher now. Before she could fully walk away, Matt caught her gaze with the full intensity of those eyes of his. Charlotte suddenly caught that Matt has said "will do" instead of "would do" and knew that whatever he was going to say next was not going to be good for her.

"Char, I am glad I caught you here. I wanted to let you know that I've taken a position with another firm. It's not patent law, but it does offer me the potential to be in a client-facing role."

"Oh really, well, that's great for you. I hope they know how lucky they are to have you. When are you going to start?"

"I put my notice in first thing this morning for two weeks. Richard hasn't said yet that he wants me to work the full-time though. I get the impression that he is considering telling me to cut it short, but he had to take another phone call so he kicked me out of his office and here I am."

"Well, you know several of the ladies around here are going to be heartbroken. Speaking of which, how's everything going with Tiffany? I assume she's excited for you."

"Ah . . . Yeah, I don't think it's going to work out with Tiffany and me."

"No? But she sounded like such a nice girl."

"Oh, she's a nice girl, but I think she actually might be too nice, you know?"

"Not really."

"Well, she never seems to have an opinion of her own. It's exhausting."

"Tiffany is, what, the sixth girl you've dated just this summer?"

"Really, it's been that many."

"Why don't you tell her that you want some time to focus on your career for a while and take some time away from the dating pool?"

"That's brilliant!"

"Well, actually I am being serious. I think it might be a good idea to get to know yourself now that you are out of school. You really don't want to rush into anything more serious."

"Charlotte, you crack me up. Half the time you sound like the sexy girl next door, and the other half of the time you sound just like my mother. I really am going to miss our talks."

"Well, just make sure you drop off your contact information before you head out."

"I'll send you a LinkedIn invitation. You are on there, right?" He batted the long eyelashes at her that no one of the male persuasion deserved to have.

"Matthew, I believe we had a conversation to continue in my office." Richard had materialized behind Charlotte, coffee cup still in hand. "Oh, and, Charlotte, I believe you have some work to attend to at your desk."

"Yes, sir." Charlotte looked sympathetically at Matt, who risked a quick smile in her direction before straightening his shoulders and following Richard back toward his lair. "Yes, the job is going to be that much duller," she thought to herself.

She sat back at her desk, opened her desk drawer, and broke open her emergency stash. "When all else fails, seek out chocolate!" Popping the morsel into her mouth, she allowed the synthetic endorphins from the delicious treat to enter into her bloodstream and power through the rest of her day.

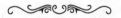

After a full day of replacing one stack of file folders with another in a seemingly endless game of hot potato, the clock struck five and Charlotte was free to make her way back to her second job. Jake was not in the mood to come quietly from day care, having decided that a game of run away from mommy was a much better use of his time. It had obviously been one of those days for his teacher as she practically threw his daily sheet at Charlotte while she attempted to round up the more adventurous preschoolers, one of which must have seen Spider-Man recently as he was attempting to climb up the classroom walls by dumping an entire jar of paste on his hands and feet.

At home an hour later, Charlotte was greeted by the sight of her husband, drenched in sweat from his ball game, yet still with an ear firmly attached to his cell phone, pacing throughout the house. This sight also meant that Charlotte was going to have to come up with some creative means of either redirecting Jake's exuberant play into another room or otherwise keeping him quiet. Of course, neither of these options were what Jake wanted to do, preferring to barrel himself at his father like a blast from a pellet gun, strewing destruction in his wake. Fletcher gave Jake a quick pat on the head before taking himself and his phone call outside. Shortly after the door closed, the oven timer started its insistent beeping.

Before the economy collapsed and Jake started to exert his own taste preferences, Charlotte had grown spoiled by arriving home to the sights and smells of decadent meals that could have been featured on foodie magazines—a perfectly seasoned pork loin with side of kale here, a brined chicken breast and saffron risotto there. Now, more often than not, their meals were a rotation of mac n' cheese, chicken nuggets, and hot dogs made even less appetizing with Charlotte acting as lead chef rather than Fletcher. Charlotte may be a whiz at fixing erratic and mysterious paper jams, but creating delicious, made-from-scratch, home-cooked meals was not one of her skills.

Charlotte peeked into the oven door as she turned off the timer. Tonight, Charlotte had been feeling fancy and had decided to branch out to frozen fish sticks. Feeling that all meals should include at least one vegetable, Charlotte dumped a can of sweet peas onto the stove and brought them to a simmer while plating the fish sticks and waiting on Fletcher to finish his call and take a quick post-game shower.

Jake decided that he would like to help this evening by opening the refrigerator, pulling out the ketchup, and pouring a third of the bottle onto his plate and the surrounding table surface. "Sorry, Mommy, I'll clean it up," announced Jake before Charlotte could get to the mess. Jake proceeded to then enhance the level of difficulty it would take to clean the mess by first creating his own version of cave painting with the excessive condiment before finally remembering what it was he originally set out to do and wiping the ketchup off the table with his hands using his shirt and his hair as a towel.

Fletcher returned to the kitchen still glued to his phone, however, at this point it was no longer attached to his ear, yet still had its tractor beam locked on Fletcher's attention. Charlotte was constantly amazed that he managed to walk around Jake's toy land mine without more incidents while his fingers frantically wiggled about the screen. As he drew closer, Charlotte noticed that the phone looked different—an upgrade, which meant a night of near-solo parenting for her as Fletcher liked to learn a new piece of technology through a marathon of trial and error rather than by reading a user manual. Charlotte had previously tried to implement a rule of no toys, including smartphones, at the table; Jake seemed to understand this rule and was good at placing his toys on the counter so that his friends could watch without getting lonely, but Fletcher was a repeat offender.

"Fletch, can you please put that away until after dinner?"

"Sure, sure, just a sec, I just have to get this out"

"Jake, honey, how was school today?

"Good."

"What did you do?"

"Um . . . You know what Angie did?"

"No, what did Angie do?"

"She tried to draw on the wall, but Ms. Thomas said that wouldn't be a good thing to do."

"No, that wouldn't be a good thing to do. What else did you do? Did you play any fun games?"

"I don't wanna talk about that right now. My tummy hurts. Can I be 'cused?"

"But you haven't eaten anything but ketchup. Can you please try to eat your fish?"

"I don't like fish." He rubbed his newly re-christened ketchup covered fingers over his face, invoking an image of a brave donning war paint.

"You haven't even tasted it."

"The fish is touching my peas. I don't like my food to touch," Jake accentuated this by flinging aside a portion of the offending fish stick.

"Please eat your dinner."

"My tummy really, really hurts"

"Jake, your tummy hurts because you are hungry. Eat your dinner."

"I said I wanted chicken nuggets!"

"Jake, eat." Charlotte did her best to invoke a tone that would inform her son that she was in no further mood for discussion.

"Dad, you supposed to put your toys away," Charlotte decided that Jake's survivor instincts must have kicked in as she listened to this long tried yet never perfected play at redirecting her attention to one of his father's supposed crimes.

"What, Jake?"

"Mom, Dad, is playing on his phone. I don't want this dinner. I want to play games too. May I please be 'cused?"

"Jake, will you please eat five big bites? Then you can be excused."

Jake held up the offending piece of fish and took a bite that barely penetrated the breading.

"One!"

"No, Jake. Big bites"

"Dad, Mom said I only have to eat five bites, and I took one and she said I still have to eat more!"

Still not looking away from his phone, Fletcher responded "Jake, eat."

Charlotte watched Jake as his expression changed to a grumpy acceptance when faced by a parental united front, his attempts to swing his dad over to his side of the argument unsuccessful, and he gradually took five rapid bites in succession, the fish pushing out his cheeks like a chipmunk hoarding nuts.

Charlotte mentally slapped herself for not demanding more bites from Jake as she witnessed the measly impact the five bites had on the content of Jake's plate, but once the bargain was set, she had to honor her side and release Jake back into the wild of the room after he washed his face and hands.

Charlotte was just sitting back down at the table when Fletcher finally finished the absolutely-cannot-wait task he was working on and returning the phone to his pocket. His entire torso heaved in a sigh as he rubbed his hand over his face.

"New phone?" asked Charlotte, knowing the answer already but taking advantage of a perfectly good conversational starter, one that was nearly guaranteed to re-engage Fletcher.

"Yeah, I just picked it up this afternoon. Somehow all my contacts are in there twice now, and I can't get my voice mail to access. It is going to take me days to get this all cleaned up."

"What was wrong with the last one?"

"Terrible service. It kept dropping my calls." Fletcher had frequently complained that his lack of service was a contributing cause for his lack of communication with the home front. Charlotte had lost track of the specific date, but she felt fairly certain that he had already switched providers at least once before for this reason alone.

"What are you going to do with the old one?"

"A few of Jake's apps still run, I think he can keep it as a toy. If not, I am organizing a cell phone for soldier's drive at the office, so if nothing else it can go in the donation pile."

"How was the rest of your day?"

"Not good. Regan is driving me nuts. She seems to have some drama going on all the time. Today she got a call that her mother had fallen or something like that and just started screaming. I wound up having to send her home. I swear some days it is a wonder that I actually get any business work done."

"If she is that much work, why do you keep her?"

"She hits her numbers."

"But she is driving you nuts."

"Yeah, but it's really hard to find someone who can do what she does for what we can afford."

"I get that, but really, if she is being constantly disruptive, is it really worth it?"

"We really can't afford not having someone bring in the leads. I'd have to do that job in addition to my own."

"Aren't you already if you are sending her home? Maybe it won't be so bad to buckle down for a while if it means finding someone else."

"You are probably right, but the timing's just not good right now. I'll have another talk with her."

Sensing that Fletcher was not really in the mood to talk about it further, Charlotte changed the subject to how her day was at the office. She could see Fletcher's eyes glaze over and then glance down to his pocket where his phone was stored. Charlotte stopped telling her story in mid-sentence just to test whether or not Fletcher was still listening. As he did not ask about the story's end, she assumed she had completely lost her audience, and they both finished their dinner; the scrape of the fork on plate and the occasional squeals from Jake in the other room punctuating the silence.

Afterward, Charlotte took Jake to the bathroom to rinse out the day's grime and the ketchup from his hair. Eventually they both reemerged, Jake fresh and clean in his fire truck pajamas, Charlotte drenched from head to foot from Jake's enthusiastic tub play. Jake took one last lap around the house retrieving Mr. Snaps, his favorite teddy bear companion from the countertop. Fletcher leaned away from his phone to give Jake a kiss on his forehead.

Stories were read, a trio of bedtime manipulation attempts were thwarted, and Charlotte mentally pictured herself slipping a card into a time clock as she turned off the light in Jake's room and closed the door.

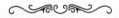

Charlotte, Fletcher, and Jake lived in a reasonably sized three-bedroom house, built back in the early nineties when high-gloss brass fixtures and small closets but open floor plans were all the rage with the builder class. The third bedroom had been converted into an art studio before Jake had been born, and Charlotte frequently would go there after all the dishes were washed and kiddo was tucked in for her own decompression from the day's stress.

Outside of the shower, this room was Charlotte's other sanctuary, albeit one that she avoided escaping to when Jake was awake. The time or two she had made that mistake, Fletcher wasn't able to keep Jake out of the room and Charlotte hadn't been able to concentrate—she lost several bottles of some of her more expensive colors but several bottles gained a purple-ly green and brown color. At one point, Charlotte and Fletcher had brought in a small child's easel for Jake. Charlotte had been overjoyed while shopping for the item, envisioning Jake dressed in an oversized smock creating mini masterpieces alongside her, giving them a chance to do something together that did not involve some combination of dirt and engines. Unfortunately, Jake had never taken to it, preferring to "help" with mommy's pieces instead. Several of her favorite pieces were "improved" during that time to include very important cars, trucks, and splotches which he claimed were airplanes.

Charlotte mostly painted for herself as a hobby; however, her friend Rhea was a fan and had requested a painting. Rhea hadn't provided any specifically requested elements, nor did she have a preferred style—for example, realism versus more contemporary—and so Charlotte was free to incorporate whatever she felt was needed in the composition. Sometimes she entered her room with a sense of purpose and theme in mind, painstakingly planning out each and every feature in the composition. Those pieces could take several days to complete, but the trade-off was the satisfaction of seeing something she had seen so clearly in her mind's eye come to reality. More often, though, she just allowed the paint to go where the mood took her; she brought form and control out of chaos which was deeply satisfying.

Tonight she was starting from a fresh canvas, its white surface open to any and all possibilities. Charlotte turned her mind off much the same way as she had earlier in the day while she had been taking notes and let the brush move across the canvas. She lost herself, focusing on the detailed strokes and colors as they filled up the blank space. Tonight, Charlotte's subconscious decided to go down the more modern art route using broad semi-translucent grays and blues that blended as excess paint dripped over a brilliant but thin red line woven throughout. These contrasts were further emphasized by indeterminable shapes of black that took on both a cavernous appearance while locking the other colors into place.

Charlotte stepped back to admire her work, hoping that Rhea would like the final result. Rhea always said she did, but Charlotte was always a little self-conscious about the quality of her artwork whenever it was going to be displayed someplace other than her art room walls. Charlotte absentmindedly wondered what had happened to the few other pieces that she had given Rhea over the past few months, surely Rhea was out of bare wall space by now. Maybe she just liked to swap them out for variety's sake. Charlotte realized that she hadn't been over to Rhea's house in ages.

Satisfied that no further work should be done to the piece, Charlotte rinsed her brushes. Several fibers fell out during the process, and Charlotte cringed, knowing this meant that she was once again in need of new supplies. After she had verified for a second time that all caps were firmly tightened on all paint jars and tubes, Jake previously demonstrating the error of neglecting that particular task, she headed to the bedroom.

Fletcher was already abed, the rapidly changing light from the television causing shadows to dance upon the walls. His eyes were closed and his breathing in the regular pattern of sleep. She had no idea how he was able to fall asleep with all the lights and the noise coming from the box, but somehow he managed, night after night. As she turned the television off, he stirred. He mumbled unintelligibly, something her previous experience led her to believe was along the lines of "Hey, I was watching that" and "Night," before shifting over to his side away from her and falling back into a deep sleep.

Chapter 2

Friendship is unnecessary, like philosophy, like art . . .
It has no survival value; rather it is one of those things
that give value to survival.

—C. S. Lewis

The following afternoon, Charlotte had arranged to meet with Rhea over lunch so that she could drop the painting off. Rhea pulled into the parking lot at nearly the same time as Charlotte, each holding up a hand in greeting to the other as they circled the fairly crowded lot for the elusive parking space near the restaurant entrance. Charlotte conceded defeat, finally finding a space around the corner from the entrance near the back of the lot. Rhea was much more successful. Charlotte struggled out of the car, trying hard not to add to the collection of pre-existing scratches and dings along the door panel, realizing that the reason the spot had been left open was due to the car in the adjacent spot double parking. Luckily she had chosen to place the painting in the trunk of the car, so getting it out undamaged was significantly easier to do.

Even though they were going to the same destination, Rhea had walked over to Charlotte's car dressed immaculately as always. In addition to being what might be considered a glamazon, Rhea had a natural grace about her. Tall, but not too tall, she was a beauty with a thin, athletic frame, creamy perfect skin, sapphire blue eyes, and a ready smile. While she always looked put together and perfect, her blond hair with its bouncy spiral curls and highlights was always in place regardless of wind or weather. To make those that didn't know her dislike her even more, she had a casual way of carrying herself that lead you to believe that she just woke up each morning looking gorgeous without spending hours struggling in the effort others took to appear merely presentable.

Charlotte knew that Rhea had come from a fairly well-to-do family, one that obviously had been wealthy for more than one generation, but far away from being considered in the top one percent. Her mannerisms and bearing never once gave off the impression of either entitlement or new money spoil. Charlotte had met Rhea in college when they joined the same study group. Charlotte had never once picked up an undercurrent of competition in their classes together as Rhea was never anything but supportive, either academically or while they were both still in the dating pool. Rhea was one of those women that other women would love to hate for her perfection if she just wasn't so sincerely nice. Hating Rhea would be pointless anyway as she would most likely thank you for the opportunity to grow as a person through experience and give you an elegantly wrapped present.

As she pulled the painting out of the trunk, Charlotte was hit again with bolt of nervous self-consciousness, unsure as to whether or not she had chosen her composition correctly, once again mentally attempting to picture the work hanging on one of Rhea's designer-inspired walls and finding it lacking. Seeing Rhea, Charlotte was made aware of how the humidity in the air had once again frizzed her hair wild and noticed that she still had some paint stuck under one of her nails from the night before. Rhea took notice of the painting, her face splitting into a happy grin.

"Oh, Charlotte, this is beautiful! I love it! You are so talented! Tell me again why you never went into art?"

"Thanks, Rhea, you know how grumpy I get when I am hungry, how in the world could I do the whole starving thing?"

"There are plenty of successful artists out there."

"Yeah, and most of them are dead. I don't do that well either."

"Well, I think you are great. Thanks for making this for me. Oh, Marie and I were talking and decided that this weekend is going to be too hot to spend in the city. Would you like to come to the beach with us for a girls' weekend? We can stay at my parent's place. I'll call Beth later on to invite her as well."

"I'll have to check with Fletcher and make sure he doesn't have anything going on. He is terrible about letting me know what his schedule is."

"Oh, I hope you can come, we really do need some relaxation time and I've got this great bottle of wine I am dying to try."

Charlotte pulled out her phone as they entered the restaurant, dialing up Fletcher who answered just before the voice mail would have picked up. Charlotte could hear quite a bit of background noise on his end, obviously he was in the middle of something.

"Sorry to bother you. Rhea invited me to her parent's place at the beach for a girls' weekend. May I go?"

"This weekend?"

"Yes, this weekend."

"Uh . . . I guess that will work." Charlotte could hear her husband begin typing in the background. She wondered if she was currently commanding enough of his attention that he might remember this call the following day. As if in answer, he threw out an unexpected follow-up statement, "Maybe I'll take Jake camping."

"Oh, he will love that!" Charlotte knew Jake would love to spend extra time in the woods with his father. A piece of Charlotte's heart frequently broke whenever she saw firsthand how elated her son would become whenever his father offered to do anything with him. His reaction wasn't quite the same as an individual returning from the desert seeing water again for the first time, but more like a dieter allowing themselves the first bite of cake after a long bout of restraint.

"Well, we'll see. Don't mention it to him. I don't want to disappoint him if we can't get away." Charlotte knew how rapidly Fletcher's plans could change, and even had Fletcher not requested that she stay silent, she definitely would not risked Jake's happiness by offering a trip only to have to take it away.

As she hung up the phone, Charlotte was practically giddy with the thought of having an entire weekend away with just the girls. No dishes to wash, no dirty clothes to pick up.

"I'm in!"

"Fantastic. I need a vacation so badly," replied Rhea as the waiter delivered her fresh field green, goat cheese, and berry salad. Charlotte could already anticipate that Rhea would only eat half of it and mentally saluted her self-control as she hungrily bit into a juicy burger.

"Me too!"

The balance of the week flew by as Charlotte anticipated getting away. Rhea's parents' beach house was only a few hours away, a drive made even easier via the recently expanded highway. Charlotte had left directly from work, having packed her bag the evening before. She had given bear hugs and kisses to Jake before dropping him off at day care, Fletcher once again scheduling himself an 8:00 a.m. presentation, promising to see him very soon. Charlotte made a quick stop by the bank along the way in order to pull out a few quick funds so that she could contribute to the wine inventory as the weekend progressed. She was dismayed to see what little balance was left, especially this shortly after her most recent payday, vowing to get a better handle on what bills were due for the balance of the month as soon as she returned.

The side of the highway gradually transitioned from field to marshland and finally to sand. As she pulled into the driveway, the sky was still bathing the area in the rosy red hue of a glorious sunset, the wind picking up a scattering of the surrounding beach and gently blasting her skin. Looking up, she could see that Rhea, Marie, and Beth had already arrived and were seated just a couple floors up on the balcony's rocking chairs, wine glasses in hand.

Marie was the first to wave, slightly sloshing the contents of her glass. Marie, normally fairly outgoing in social settings, never meeting a stranger provided she was in a comfortable setting, simply thrived in a beach existence as if the sea air in her lungs gave her an extra boost of energy. When she moved, her gestures were always exuberant as if she constantly lived at a party and large, wild gestures were the only way to capture another's attention in a crowd. The sea breeze whipped her straight dark brown hair. Marie had a thin frame similar to Rhea, though hers was more caused by her natural day-to-day burning of energy rather than the defined muscular tone of regular athletic activity. Marie was the type to devour a pizza when the mood hit, go out dancing, and then sleep through breakfast and occasionally lunch the next day. Luckily for her, she had found a job that allowed for flexible hours: she could work a twelve-hour day one day, followed by a four-hour day the next, provided that by the end of the week she had put in at least the full forty hours total. There were many days Charlotte yearned for a similar existence, especially on those days with blue skies and temperatures in the midseventies.

Beth, in contrast, was nearly the polar opposite of Marie, her short curly hair bouncing in the breeze as she nodded her head in way of greeting. Beth was a couple years older than Marie, who was a year older than both Rhea and Charlotte. Her gray eyes calm with a maturity about her that went beyond her biological years. Beth was the group's rock—solid and supportive. While not obese, her edges were rounder than the others, but she seemed to be more than comfortable with her own skin, a trait that Charlotte envied and admired. Beth had a sense of stability about her, a natural aura of responsibility, which most likely had helped to balance out Marie's wildness before anyone got into trouble through the years. Beth had chosen to marry an older man with a child from a previous marriage and no interest in further expanding his family. Beth seemed to accept that she would not be changing diapers from her own natural child, her step-child half grown, rarely visiting, and had instead frequently helped out with the rest of the group's babies as needed.

"You got here just in time!" exclaimed Marie, shouting down toward Charlotte. "Hurry up here, we're just opening another bottle!" This was most likely a timely action as Charlotte noticed more liquid launch itself from Marie's glass.

"Do you need help bringing in your things?" asked Beth. The house consisted of two floors, well, four floors if you counted the rec room positioned on the ground level between the support pillars and the exterior shower and the widow's walk at the top. It had multiple entrances which could be reached by spiraling up a twisted exterior stairwell. Charlotte never minded the climb. The view up top where her friends were positioned was spectacular.

"How was the drive down for you?" asked Rhea.

"Do I need to pick up a glass from inside? No, Beth, I can carry it all. Traffic was fine. How was it for you?"

"Ugh, you can answer all that when you get up here! I'll have your glass ready!"

Marie thrust a wine-filled glass into Charlotte's hand the minute she was through the sliding glass door. Beth had brought an additional seat over and sat in it, allowed Charlotte to be centered within the group on the balcony. Charlotte noticed that music was playing on a small boom box in the corner typical of the older electronics that many people leave at beach homes which are rented out when not in use by the property's owners.

"Have I ever mentioned how much I appreciate your parents' letting us use this space, Rhea?"

"It's no problem at all. They haven't had a ton of renters this season, more than the last couple of years, but still not like they had five years ago. They are considering selling it."

Marie's attention was immediately captured by that statement. "No! They can't sell! This place is awesome! Where would we go when we had to get away? Charlotte, I guess you'd have to get us a place after Fletcher has made his millions."

Beth snorted, "Yes, Charlotte, no pressure."

"No pressure at all," responded Charlotte as she sipped from her wine and watched the last of the sunlight's rays reflect off the ocean waves and eventually replaced altogether by starlight. Charlotte was always amazed at how leisurely the sun began its descent but how the light seemed to pop like a soap bubble the minute the sun touched the horizon line, especially at the beach.

"So anyway, as I was telling these guys," began Marie, "Yesterday, I asked Tom if we could hire a cleaning service to help out once in a while. Not every week, just someone to help clean the baseboards. You would think that I was asking for a pile of gold. I tried to convince him it was a great idea, explaining the amount of time it would allow us to spend as a family on the weekend if I didn't have to clean all day Sunday. He said he didn't mind the dirty floors. How can he not mind the dirty floors? Doesn't he know how stressed out a dirty house makes me?"

"Oh, a cleaning service would be awesome. I can only imagine how lovely it would be to come home at the end of the day to a house where everything smells clean. I think it is definitely worth the expense. In fact, tell Tom that I want one too!" agreed Charlotte who also spent a good portion of her Sunday scrambling to fit in as much cleaning as possible during Jake's nap time—provided that Jake actually took a nap. Currently the dust bunnies were winning that particular war.

"Yeah, Tom is just being Tom again. I swear, the man could teach Fort Knox lessons in currency protection. It's not like I am asking for something we can't afford, but he makes it sound like we would be applying for food stamps next."

"Brian is not a huge fan of my horseback riding either," chimed in Rhea. Rhea and Brian were married before Charlotte and Rhea had graduated college—together longer than any of the other couples in the group. Even so, Charlotte didn't know Brian all that well as he typically avoided Rhea's "Ladies' Functions" as one might attempt to avoid a passenger on a subway possessing a nervous tic, a hacking cough, and involved in a heated conversation with himself or herself. Although she attempted to give him the benefit of the doubt, Charlotte's opinion of him was predominately shaped by Rhea's contributions to their regular gossip and venting sessions. That is to say, in Charlotte's opinion, Brian was much like a male nipple. She clearly accepted that he wasn't going anywhere and recognized that he most likely filled some vital evolutionary purpose, but what that purpose might be was a mystery to Charlotte. Rhea never seemed to be overly concerned about the separation her husband had placed on her social and married life, or if she did, she hid it well with the same natural grace that accentuated everything she did. The only real public evidence of their marriage beyond the occasional photographs that looked like they could have come with the picture frame was their son, aged ten, a son Rhea would obviously walk over coals for.

"I've been volunteering at the stable with a group offering equine therapy for needy teens, and our group was being honored by the city over a dinner with the mayor. It might have even been on the local news, I didn't check. We could bring a guest, but Brian wasn't all that interested. Besides, you know how hard it can be to find a last-minute sitter." Charlotte did. It was one of the many reasons she and Fletcher rarely went out. "I had bought this great new dress and must have spent two hours getting ready. I came out of the room, and Brian was sitting on the couch watching his baseball game. He didn't even look up. Lance came in and said, 'Mom, you look beautiful! Doesn't she, Dad?' He was so stern when he said it. It was like he was trying to scold his dad for not standing up when I entered the room. It was so hilarious. My little man is growing into such a gentleman. I've been told he runs around opening doors for the girls in his class at school too."

Beth looked toward Charlotte and asked, "So, Ms. Birthday Girl, obviously you are celebrating with us, but did Fletcher or Jake do anything to help you celebrate at home?"

Charlotte cringed internally, not particularly wanting to be either reminded of her advancing years, but also slightly ashamed to admit that she and Fletcher hadn't done anything in particular to commemorate the day. "Um, Jake made me a card at day care, but nothing special. We decided to take it easy instead." Charlotte wasn't lying to her friends, neither she nor Fletcher had been in a celebratory mood that night, but she did gloss over the full truth. Fletcher had been particularly distracted, and Charlotte had been depressed, convinced that Fletcher actually would have forgotten it altogether had Jake not mentioned it that evening at dinner. At the same time, money was tight, so it probably wasn't the worst thing for their finances to avoid extra expenditures on gifts, babysitters, and an unnecessary night of entertainment.

The stories continued well into the night, and the bag they had brought along to collect their recyclables grew heavy. Nearly all the stories bemoaned some aspect of the teller's daily life, whether it was work, extended family members, kids, or spouses. A few of the unwritten rules of Ladies' Nights Out gossip were never criticize another's spouse and never offer unsolicited advice, such as advocating a life change. These exchanges were merely designed as a means to vent personal frustrations safely. Each participant could leave the evening feeling like they were not alone in their relationship challenges. Beth chose to participate by making sure everyone was hydrated and fed so that no one had reason to regret the evening before; however, she rarely offered her own personal stories. Charlotte did not know whether it was a case of Beth just not being one to air her dirty laundry or if her husband had learned enough from the mistakes of his first marriage to avoid them the second time around. Charlotte suspected it could be a combination of the two.

Lately though, Charlotte had been growing somewhat depressed by these exchanges. For several years, she would throw in the occasional tidbit, but would return home secretly smug that her worst story was better than many of the others' best stories. She would return home content and curl up beside Fletcher on the couch and would share some of the juiciest stories. Now, when she arrived home afterward, Fletcher was frequently locked away in front of his computer or similarly checked out in front of his phone. She could only imagine what her friends were telling their own significant others about her and Fletcher when they returned home.

In more recent months, she had found herself becoming quieter with her friends, not willing to potentially tempt one of the ladies into inadvertently breaking the rules. Occasionally, Charlotte would think back to what their conversations used to be like before there were spouses to roll your eyes about or before a good third of the conversation dealt with children's various bodily fluids and functions. Her friends used to discuss movies and books which didn't involve cartoon characters or were thinly veiled ninety-minute commercials for action figures. They used to discuss career aspirations or what was more attractive, abs or buns.

The rest of the weekend was absolutely glorious for Charlotte. The sun shone, the water was warm, and Charlotte was gratified to see that she had timed her exposure to the elements perfectly—her skin bronzed without even a hint of sunburn. At one point, she had smugly thought to herself that a young group of guys down the beach had been eyeballing her and enjoyed feeling like a hot momma, only to realize that what they were looking at was her hair. It had outdone itself, half escaping from the band she had attempted to hold it back, resulting in a partial halo of frizz surrounding a wannabe flock of seagulls send up. Marie had been nice enough to call her attention to it when she had commented to the others about her potential fan club. It was going to be a nightmare to detangle, and Charlotte once again flirted with the idea of hacking it all off and dealing with the consequences later.

Eventually, though, it was time to clean up the house and pack up the car. Everyone thanked Rhea for arranging the outing, and if Charlotte took a little longer to vacuum the sand up from the carpeting and further delay her start home, no one chose to say anything. Charlotte volunteered to drive Beth home, which would further extend the amount of time it would take to arrive home.

Mentally bracing herself for the inevitable chaos that would be meeting her at the house, Charlotte slowly drove the last few miles home after dropping Beth off, savoring the last minutes of "off time." She pulled into the driveway, turned off the car, and sat in silence, taking some deep breaths as way of preparation. A few moments later, Charlotte had her game face back on and opened the door to the house, her eyes closed as if to spare herself from the mess that she knew would be there demanding her immediate attention.

Chapter 3

How did it get so late so soon? Its night before its afternoon. December is here before its June. My goodness how the time has flewn. How did it get so late so soon?

—Dr. Seuss

She had expected to be met by a rabid four-year-old barreling into her waist exclaiming "Mommy, Mommy, Mommy!" When that didn't immediately occur, she looked back out into the garage and noticed that Fletcher's car wasn't there. She hadn't really been paying attention when she first came in, so mentally focused on delaying the inevitable.

She must have beaten them home and would be granted a few more precious minutes of me time. Upon entry, she noted that there were a few toys scattered about—actually, the house appeared unusually clean for a weekend without her. Fletcher and Jake must not have been in residence much. With a sigh

42

of guilty relief, Charlotte brought her bag into house, emptying the contents into the laundry where they joined a few other garments waiting for the next load to be run. She took a quick shower to get the last of the sand off her body, noticing that there was a large gap in the amount of clothing in Fletcher's closet. "He must have decided to go camping after all," she thought to herself. Once dressed and hair dried, she returned to the kitchen to see if Fletcher had left a note indicating where he may have gone and when they might have returned. She was unsurprised to see that he hadn't.

Charlotte decided to take advantage of the bonus time and queued up a chick flick that had been patiently waiting on her Netflix list for several months. She could hear the buzzer of the washing machine just as the couple on the screen parted ways over the expected over-the-top misunderstanding. The clothes were tumbling away in the dryer as the male lead realized how he could not live without the female lead, causing a public spectacle and somehow avoiding arrest as he professed his undying love. These movies may be formulaic, but the formula is there because it works, and Charlotte began to tear up over their perfect happiness.

The credits rolled without a phone call from Fletcher saying their estimated time of arrival. Charlotte decided that she had had enough waiting around for the boys to call and dialed Fletcher's cell. It rang through to his voice mail without answer. Charlotte decided that Fletcher must have taken their son camping somewhere with spotty cell phone reception and

Allie Potts

mentally berated him for doing so. She called over to Marie's house.

"Hi, Marie, it's Charlotte. Hey, is Tom there?"

"Yeah, he's here. Do you need me to get him?" Charlotte overheard Marie shouting on her end of the line calling for her husband Tom, who was also conveniently Fletcher's best friend.

"Oh, I thought he might have gone camping with Fletcher and Jake."

"They went camping? How fun!"

"I think so, but there is no note, so I am not sure. Maybe he mentioned something to Tom?"

"Tom! Tom! It's Charlotte!" Charlotte had to pull the phone away from her ear briefly in an effort to protect her hearing. Tom must have somehow avoided Marie's initial call to him, and Marie must have forgotten to reposition the phone's microphone as this was a direct assault on her senses. "Did Fletcher go camping?"

Charlotte could hear some mumbling in the background that must be Tom's reply.

"Tom hasn't heard from Fletcher since last week."

"Oh. Okay. Thanks."

"Aren't guys great communicators?"

"Oh yes. Well, thanks. I guess I will just have to wait around for him to get back."

"All right, I hope you give him an earful when you see him. Great seeing you this weekend. We need to do it again soon!"

"Yes, we do! Bye!"

"Bye!"

Not wanting to spoil her appetite, though recognizing that hunger was going to quicken her speed to anger, Charlotte made herself a small snack as she waited for the clothes dryer to finish its cycle. Laundry sorted and folded, Charlotte brought a small pile into Jake's room. As she opened the drawer, she was puzzled to see that all of Jake's clothes had been removed. She opened the closet, the hangers in there too had been stripped and a few toys were missing from the bed.

"How many nights did he think he was packing for?" she asked herself.

Charlotte glanced up and saw that up in the topmost corner of the closet, wedged almost out of sight, was Jake's sleeping bag. The annoyance she had been attempting to squash in the pit of her stomach began to be replaced by doubt flavored with a hint of fear.

"Maybe Fletcher couldn't remember where we stored it. Maybe he figured they would just sleep on top of blankets. It's been warm."

She went back out to the garage. There, sitting on top of the shelving unit, was their tent still in the same position it had been since Fletcher's last camping trip several months ago.

Charlotte ran back over to the phone and dialed Fletchers number again. Voice mail answered on the second ring.

"Hi, Fletcher. It's me. I'm back from my trip. Umm, I thought you were going to go camping, but I see the tent is still here. Where are you? Call me!"

Charlotte redialed and was met with the same result. Charlotte called her mom.

"Hi, Mom, it's Charlotte."

"Hi, sweetie! I was just thinking about you. Your sister is going to be coming into town in just a couple of weeks, and we were thinking about going to see a musical. Now I know that money is tight for you, so don't you worry, it would be my treat!"

Charlotte cringed as she did whenever her mom made mention of their financial situation. She hated that her mother knew how tight things were; she knew that her mother secretly believed that she and Fletcher sacrificed too much, but additionally Charlotte felt guilty. Her mom should be saving her money for her own nearing retirement, not throwing it out in support of her adult children, especially not for frivolous things. "That's Okay, Mom. Um . . . Mom? Is Jake with you?"

"No, Honey. Why? What's going on?"

"Fletcher said he might go camping with Jake this weekend while I was at the beach with some friends, but he didn't take the tent or Jake's sleeping bag. But Jake's clothes are missing, so I thought that maybe he had some crisis at work and had to drop Jake off for the weekend with you."

"Oh goodness. No, honey. I haven't heard from them at all."

"How is Fletcher's work? What kind of crisis might there be?"

"You know how it goes. There is always some sort of emergency he has to travel to. Maybe he decided to take Jake with him this time. I know he doesn't want to bother you."

"Jake is never a bother."

"I guess I'll just wait to hear from him a little bit longer."

"Well, you let me know when you do!"

"Okay. Bye, Mom."

"Bye. Oh, and let me know if you change your mind about those tickets! Remember, my treat!"

Charlotte fought her growing paranoia by fixing herself a more complete meal of leftovers. "They will have picked something up for themselves along the way." She queued up another of her stored chick flicks, though turned it off after only a few minutes, the program not sufficiently distracting her from her thoughts.

The phone rang a few times as the evening progressed. Each time, Charlotte progressively raced faster to pick it up, only to hear the distinctive click of the line being connected to a ready-in-waiting telemarketer. Charlotte lost even the semblance of good manners as she hung up on them in order to clear the line for a call from Fletcher.

The sky darkened, and Charlotte attempted to distract herself by painting, then readying for the workday tomorrow. Unable to decide what emotion best described her state of being, a combination of anger and fear continuing to war in her belly, Charlotte knew that Fletcher's voice mail must now be close to full as at least five of the messages were from her. She attempted to wait up for them, but eventually succumbed to sleep, book in hand and nightstand lamp still burning, her company only the ticking from the clock in the hall.

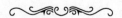

The alarm clock blared, startling Charlotte back into semi-wakefulness; she reached over to gently nudge Fletcher awake so that he could turn off the sound, her arm falling onto an empty mattress. The last fragments of sleep blazed away as she realized that Fletcher was still not there. She sat frozen in indecision. If Fletcher truly was called away for an emergency over the weekend without calling or leaving a note, then he was a dead man the minute he arrived home; and it was most likely best for the health of all if she went about her day like usual so that he could at least wallpaper the house with flowers and expensive gifts while she was at work. She hardly wished to think about alternative possibilities, afraid that if she even thought about them, they could somehow come true.

"If they got into an accident, I should be at home so that the doctors can reach me," she thought to herself. "What if they have been trying to reach me while I was on the beach!" She raced to her cell phone, dialing her voice mail. The robotic voice announced "No new messages" as she had repeatedly done the evening before.

Unsatisfied, Charlotte called all three of the major hospitals to determine if patients had been brought in matching her husband and son's description, with no success. She then scrolled through the local news stations to see if there were any reports of traffic accidents or other incidents with similar results. The top news story was the results of a local pie eating contest, informing Charlotte that the news had been relatively light over the weekend. She took a small degree of comfort in the belief that an event causing harm to her four-year-old would have taken precedence and must not have occurred.

Fletcher's employees would not start arriving at the office for another hour. Determined that sitting around the house waiting was only going to make her crazy, Charlotte decided that she would at least attempt to go to work. She readied herself for the day without closing the bathroom door, stopping the flow of water each time she thought she heard a phone ring, afraid that she might not reach it in time; otherwise, she was already preparing the verbal berating that Fletcher was due for causing her to worry. "How hard is it to leave a note!"

Charlotte attempted to put on her make-up, a process made more difficult as the skin below her eyes now showed the gray bags of unproductive sleep. She found herself sobbing, ruining what little progress she had made. "Get yourself together. They are fine. He always has a story. He's probably decided to take Jake straight to day care and went directly to work. He is going to show up later today and accuse you of overreacting, and you need to work through lunch the rest of the week to make up for all the time you are wasting this morning."

Pep talk completed, Charlotte finished getting herself ready and took a detour toward Jake's day care. "I'll just pop in to make sure he had a good weekend." Jake's day care was equipped with a child check-in system at the front desk. Each parent was given a code which they used to sign a child in or out. The child's name is shown in green when they were present, and shown in red when they left for the day.

The receptionist tilted her head in questioned greeting when Charlotte opened the door. "Good morning. We weren't sure if we were going to see Jake today."

"He's not here?"

"You're not dropping him off?"

Charlotte punched in her code, Jake's name appearing in red, confirming that he was not in attendance. Unwilling to share her concerns, afraid of crying once again, Charlotte decided to avoid the whole truth.

"His dad is dropping him off, but I missed saying goodbye to him this morning and was hoping to surprise him. I guess they must have stopped for breakfast along the way."

"Aren't you a good mom. You are welcome to wait over here. Have some coffee."

"No, that's Okay. I will see him when I pick him up later."

"All right. You have a great day!"

"You too."

Charlotte returned to the car. "I'm not going to cry. I'm not going to cry. They are having breakfast somewhere on their way back."

Somehow, Charlotte's muscle memory powered the car to her office parking lot. She managed to log into to her computer, but little else. Richard completed his attendance circuit, the level of his coffee cup showing that he had already completed multiple laps before she arrived. Charlotte didn't waste effort caring. His lips thinned in displeasure. "I said, good morning, Charlotte." Charlotte hadn't heard the first time he said the phrase, he may have even said it more than once, and she muttered a reply in order to give him the acknowledgement he needed to walk away.

The second he was out of hearing distance, she dialed her husband's office—a frowned-upon personal call.

"Archer Service Solutions."

"Um, yes, this is Charlotte. Is Fletcher there?"

"Hi, Charlotte! No, sorry hon, he's not. Do you want me to forward you to his cell phone?"

"Did he happen to mention an emergency that would make him travel out of town over the weekend?"

"Not to me, but I took most of last week off. Is everything Okay?"

"I'm just trying to track him down."

"Do you want to talk to Daniel? I'll transfer you."

After a few seconds of easy listening hold music, Charlotte heard the distinctive click of the call connecting. "Daniel?"

"Hi, Charlotte. What can I do for you?"

"I am trying to track down Fletcher. He's not answering his cell phone. Do you know where he might be?"

"Sorry, I don't. There are a few prospects on the board that he might be meeting with today though."

"Did he happen to mention an emergency that would cause him to travel over the weekend?"

"He didn't, but I was out making sales calls myself on Friday. This is actually the first time I've been physically in the office for the past few days."

"Okay. Well, when he checks in, would you please ask him to call me?"

"Sure, will do."

Charlotte returned the phone to its cradle. She had been facing down toward her desk, her elbow resting on the desk surface, her temple resting on her hand during the call. Richard must have returned from behind her as she was met with his an expression of displeasure. "I have a call with a client two minutes ago. I need you in my office now."

The morning passed without any update from Fletcher or Fletcher's office. Richard returned to her desk around lunch time.

"Charlotte, I must say I am disappointed with you. A woman of your age should not be partying that hard over the weekend. I think you should go home and sleep it off."

Charlotte sputtered incredulously, "You think I'm hungover?"

"You did mention to my assistant that you were going to the beach this weekend with your friends, did you not?"

"Well, yes, but that's not what's going on at all."

"Charlotte, I require all my staff to demonstrate professionalism at all times. Our clients need to know that all staff members from the front desk to the back office are dedicated to them and only them."

"I'm worried about my son and my husband!"

"That does sound like a personal problem. One that I think is best you attend to outside of the office. As I said, go home. You may come back tomorrow when you are focused again on our clients."

As demeaning as the message was delivered, Charlotte had to concede that Richard had made a valid point. She wasn't focused on her work, as she pressed the save button before closing out her work, she noted at least a dozen typos on the screen.

With her hand on the car door, Charlotte also decided she could no longer ignore the small voice that had been nagging her for the past twenty-four hours. She was going to have to file a missing persons report with the police. She just hoped that this was going to be one of those incidents she and Fletcher could laugh about later.

Chapter 4

Denial ain't just a river in Egypt.

—Mark Twain

As Charlotte sat in the yellowing plastic chairs that lined the police station waiting area, she wondered for the tenth time what she was doing there. "This is going to be a waste of my time. I bet he is walking through the door at home like there is nothing wrong in the world while am stuck here. Jake will probably be on a sugar high, and Fletcher will tell some story about Jake accidentally dropping the phone in a cooler or leaving it on top of the car. I should just get up and leave," she thought to herself.

Charlotte glanced down the row of seats joined together with singular bar. A middle-aged woman sat on the far end of the row, worrying over a small photograph with dog-eared edges. "I don't even have a current photograph of them," she realized. Charlotte and Fletcher had wholeheartedly embraced the low cost and convenience of digital photography. Their last professional pictures had been taken when Jake was still in diapers. "Hopefully they will be able to accept a digital transfer photo."

Across the room sat a couple clinging together as if they were each other's sole life raft in a sea of trouble. Near them sat another woman who, unlike the others, had a look of a lifetime of experience, her expression a storm. Charlotte pitied whoever might be attached to that woman currently protected by a holding cell. The minute hand on the analog clock on the wall continued its forward progress.

The officer at the window waved Charlotte over, "What are you here for?"

"Um, I think I need to file a missing persons report."

"How long has he or she been missing?"

"I'm not quite sure. At least twenty-four hours, maybe as many as four days?"

"And who is missing?"

"My husband and my son."

"Does your husband suffer from any form of mental condition that could in any way impact his judgment?"

"No."

"And do you have any reason to suspect that there was any sort of foul play or otherwise suspicious circumstances contributing to their disappearance?"

"No. I mean, maybe? I don't know?"

"What is the age of your son?'

"Four."

"I'll need you to complete this form as completely as possible. Do you have a photograph?"

"Only on my phone. Can you use that?"

The officer squished her features, annoyed. "Do you have a USB cord or other form of transfer device?"

"No, I guess I didn't think this through."

"Well, return to your seat and complete the form so that we can get started. When you are done, please bring the form and the clipboard back up to me. You'll need to have a photo ready when the police officer assigned follows up with you once the investigation is under way."

Charlotte returned to her seat, pen and clipboard in hand. She stared at the questionnaire. She realized in a panic that she couldn't answer even basic questions like what they were wearing when they were last seen. She tried to think back to Friday morning, which now seemed like ages ago. Jake had been wearing what, the blue shirt she liked so much because it brought out the color of his eyes? No, he had wanted to dress like his dad again that morning. They both were wearing red that morning. That's right, Jake had his red polo shirt on, the one with the button that refused to remain in place, the collar turned slightly up. He had his khaki shorts on, the ones that were too wide around the waist and sagged down upon his hips, but the ones he liked so much because they resembled his dad's work slacks. His brown hair had been matted down on one side from sleeping hard the night before, his bangs sweeping up desperately in need of another haircut. Charlotte was planning on whipping out the scissors for an at-home cheap trim later this week. This meant that Fletcher must also be wearing his red polo shirt and tan slacks, a pairing that he would not have worn if he was planning a number of first-time prospective sales calls.

Charlotte returned the form to the window and continued to wait, preferring to watch the minute hand of the clock shift rather than meet the eyes of the other people on the benches. Every so often, one would change. The angry woman replaced with a greasy overweight man with scraggy beard who smelled of cheap alcohol, the terrified couple replaced with an aloof teen, blaring music through his ear buds.

"Mrs. Row?" An officer stood in the doorway to the waiting area, glancing down at a clipboard and then scanning the individuals in the room. Charlotte quickly gathered her things as she slightly raised her hand at him to signify her attendance. "This way."

They passed a few desks with other officers in the process of either conducting interviews or processing paperwork. "Have a seat, Mrs. Row."

"It says here that you are reporting both your husband and your son missing. Is this correct?"

"Yes."

"And that they may have been missing as many as four days?"

"Yes, um, I went to the beach with friends directly after work on Friday and didn't come back until Sunday afternoon?"

"And you never checked in with your family during your trip?"

"No. It was supposed to be a girls-only weekend. No phones."

"And why, if you returned on Sunday, are you only reporting their disappearance at—" he looked at the clock, "4:15 on Monday?"

"My husband said that he might take them camping while I was gone. He is terrible about letting me know when his plans change or if he gets delayed."

"And you don't believe he's merely gone for a long weekend with your son?"

"The tent and my son's sleeping bag are still in the house."

"So if you don't think they went camping, why did you not report the disappearance yesterday?"

"My husband runs his own business and has to travel quite a bit last minute. I thought that maybe he had an emergency come up and had to take Jake with him."

"And you no longer think that?"

"I called his office this morning and no one there seems to know anything."

"And there was nothing out of place at your home? Windows intact? No sign of forced entry? No notes of any kind?"

"Everything at the house seemed fine. There were a few toys scattered around, but that's not unusual for a weekend at our house, especially if I haven't been there. As far as I can tell, the only things missing were nearly Jake's entire summer wardrobe, some of Fletcher's clothes, and Fletcher's car." The officer who had been jotting her comments down as they had been speaking put his pen down. He leaned in, gradually, almost regretfully making eye contact.

"Mrs. Row, would you describe your marriage as happy?"

Charlotte reflexively started to reply with "Of course!" Only, as soon as the words were partially out of her mouth, did she realize that she could no longer honestly say the words with quite as much conviction as she felt she ought to.

"I mean, I think it is. Err, I mean, we have the same up and downs that all couples have. The last six months or so," or maybe longer than that, Charlotte thought to herself, "haven't been necessarily stellar, but Fletcher has been so stressed out about work and we haven't really gotten to go out very much." She actually couldn't recall the last time they had gone out for a real grown-up date at all. Charlotte's mother always offered to babysit, but there had been so many times when Richard would demand Charlotte to stay late at work and Fletcher forced to soothe a customer and they had no choice but to beg for assistance from her mom that Charlotte felt guilty asking her mom to help out when it wasn't critical.

Charlotte couldn't remember the last time they had been intimate. When they first had gotten married, they would lean in, kiss each other, and tell each other "I love you" at every traffic light. Now, the few times they traveled in a car together, Fletcher would take advantage of the traffic light to send e-mails and text messages in rapid fire—a practice that Charlotte had asked him to stop at least while she was in the car, but one that was fairly unavoidable for the self-employed.

Forget about sex. The last few attempts had been halfhearted at best, both of them seeming to want to go to sleep more than to become physical with each other.

"And why would Fletcher be stressed out about work?"

Charlotte attempted to explain to the officer about Fletcher losing his previous job and his declaration that he never will be dependent on another company again. He had been a software engineer with a firm that specialized in helping newly acquired companies migrate to the systems utilized by their new parent organizations. This was during the time when loans were cheap and everyone was in acquisition mode. When the banking crisis took hit, the firm changed its focus to helping companies further automate their processes while they downsized or closed operating sites outright. Eventually, his own firm was forced to shed its workforce, leaving many with limited options.

She explained how he was going to develop and sell a product that brought real value to customers, and how he was going to treat his own employees with more respect than he was showed. He wanted to be a job creator.

"So business isn't doing so great."

"Why would you say that?"

"Mrs. Row, I am sure that your husband started out with the best of intentions, but from where I sit, it is really hard to make money and keep your ideals."

"It can be done."

"Eh," the officer shrugged, "Maybe it can. I am just saying that in my experience, I've seen a number of good and decent people struggling to make ends meet, while we've been called in to forcibly remove a number of angry former employees of big businesses screaming about how their former bosses wronged or cheated them. They might be right, but we have to remove them anyway because they are trespassing, and the law is the law." Charlotte had no response to the officer's observation, and was disheartened that she couldn't immediately call up a number of examples to disprove his theory.

The officer continued, "Describe your personal finances."

"Well . . . things have been tight. We really thought things with his company would have taken off quicker, but they say that every overnight success takes five years." Charlotte nervously chuckled. She was never comfortable discussing their financial situation. "We've put ourselves on a budget, and we get by."

"Anything stored away that someone else might know about or see of value?"

"Er . . . no. Nothing beyond a couple week's savings. Most everything we have has been invested into his business."

"Everything? You don't even have any savings or retirement funds of your own?"

"Everything. I wanted to support his dream."

"And you've not received any return on that investment yet? Nothing at all that a potential kidnapper would believe be available for ransom?"

"No," replied Charlotte, extremely uncomfortable at this point, additionally feeling ashamed and slightly foolish.

"Mrs. Row. I am going to level with you. Based on what you've told me, it does not sound like a third party had anything to gain from the disappearance of your family, and barring accident or other act of nature, it sounds highly likely that your husband has taken your son away with a degree of advanced planning. If it was only your husband, I cannot honestly say that we would extend a number of resources into this investigation, but because there is a minor involved, we will place a few calls ourselves. Additionally, we will put out a notice describing the vehicle, your son, and your husband. But Mrs. Row, understand that there is a good possibility that he has already put several miles between you, and it is highly unlikely that we will get a hit on any bulletin issued tonight. We will need a current photograph from you. I understand that you do not have one at this time, here's my e-mail address. If you would, when you get home, please send me the picture and I'll update the file. If evidence is found that they've crossed state lines, the matter may get escalated to the federal level, however, that is not a sure thing. It might also be a good idea for you to also meet with a private investigator."

"What are you saying exactly?" Charlotte asked, but deep down already anticipated the next words out of the officer's mouth.

"Mrs. Row, I am saying that I believe your husband saw an opportunity to make a clean start somewhere else, has abducted your son, and has no intention on coming back."

Parental Child Abduction. Charlotte understood each of those words as they stood alone, but combined together to describe her situation just did not make any sense at all. The officer continued speaking, but Charlotte's brain could no longer translate the sounds coming from his mouth into meaningful words. What the officer was suggesting could not possibly apply to her. That was the sort of thing that happened to other people. She knew that she and Fletcher had been drifting apart recently, and yes, they hadn't been having a number of honest conversations with each other lately, but surely he wouldn't have felt the need to run away under cover of darkness; and even more certainly, he wouldn't deny her access to Jake.

She drove home in a daze. Already the signs on the highway started to blaze with the message "Amber Alert." How many times had she seen those signs since the DOT started to use them, absentmindedly thinking about how terrible it must be for those families while also thinking about what might be for dinner, rarely looking at the cars around her to see if they might match the description.

The police officer had mentioned a private investigator. It was almost as if he was suggesting that there wasn't going to be much the police department was going to be able to do. Unfortunately, as she had mentioned to the officer, Charlotte didn't exactly have a large chunk of available funds to help pay for the investigation.

Voices of self-doubt continued to speak in her mind. One part of her continued to refuse to accept that her family's absence was anything other than the tragically overblown misunderstandings like she regularly viewed in her romantic comedies. There was still the possibility that she would pull into the driveway and see here family inside, having wondered where in the world she had been all day. She could even picture it in glorious detail: Jake getting red in the face, accusing her of forgetting to pick him up from day care, Fletcher stirring a pot of mac n' cheese in one hand, phone in the other. She would tell Jake that she was a silly mommy, and they would hug and laugh. Later, she and Fletcher would get into an argument about how neither of them left a note about the their comings and goings, and though she would go to bed that night annoyed immensely with him, at least she could go to bed secure knowing that her family was all in their proper places and that life would return to normal tomorrow.

The other voice did not paint as blissful a picture. That voice showed her a picture of the police finding the car in a ditch halfway between their house and the nearby indoor waterpark. This particular voice offered an alternative destination for Fletcher and Jake to go to for father and son time that did not require a tent or sleeping bag. In this vision, Fletcher's car smoldered, only a shell of the vehicle remaining, the side of the car missing from where the jaws of life were used to disengage the door from the frame. Blankets covered the burnt and unidentified bodies of the tragic victims as they are loaded in a van destined for the morgue.

The third voice took the police officer's suggestion and ran with it. In this vision, which was brighter than all the others, was nearly glaringly cartoonish. It showed that Fletcher drove off into the sunset, his arms around a tiny-waisted, busty blonde covered in jewelry—paid for by her money—explaining to Jake in the backseat that this woman was his new, better mommy, and how they were going to embark on an adventure! Charlotte's subconscious didn't care to answer questions like where in the world would Fletcher have met such a woman. And while she couldn't be sure that he hadn't drained their bank account dry, the available funds most assuredly couldn't have covered the cost of the woman's jewels, so where would the extra money have come from?

Charlotte entered her home. She picked up a couple of Jake's toys from where they lay around the parameter of the den and began to return them to their assigned nooks and cubbies. The toy in her hand was a large-sized fire truck with authentic working sounds that her mother had given Jake last year. Jake had decided that he was going to grow up to be a fireman and, upon receipt, had pushed the buttons repeatedly until Charlotte and Fletcher had been left with no choice but to strategically hide the toy away. Jake had a nose like a bloodhound's for the truck, and no matter where it was stored, he always found it—triumphantly returning it to its place of glory in the center of the den. The batteries were now nearly worn out, with Charlotte pressing one of the buttons without thinking, and the resulting siren was a low pitiful wail as if the toy was dying.

Christmas had snuck up on the family last year, whether it was due to the unseasonably warm weather or just the fact that life had picked up in speed. Their normal Christmas spending had been reduced to only a few gifts for Jake, such as a much smaller and much quieter fire truck, and only one or two items that they felt the other parent truly needed. Charlotte had bought the toy only days ago and had been so proud of herself for finding such a perfect gift, on sale, for her son.

Charlotte's mother had arrived before the coffee even cooled, the trunk of her car more closely matching a young boy's vision of the back of Santa's sleigh. Fletcher had whispered to her mother that she had spent too much, to which Charlotte's mother had replied, "Kids need toys at Christmas!" Charlotte herself was unsure if her mother was just being overly generous that particular day or if she was making a more subtle statement, implying that Fletcher and Charlotte were not adequately providing for her grandson.

Bits of paper launched themselves into the air as Jake had devoured present after present, finally opening the box containing the fire truck. His movement finally stilled as he took it all in. He pushed the button for the first time, filling the room with the siren destined to go on repeat for the next six months. Then without prompting, he had run over, grabbed the small truck his parents had given him, placing them both together, announcing to everyone that he now had both the mommy truck and the son truck and they were going to save people together. He then completed a circuit in the room, throwing his little body at each of the grown-ups in full hug abandon. In the face of such pure and innocent joy, neither Charlotte nor Fletcher could remain irritated with her mother's gesture. Fletcher had put his arm around her shoulders as they watched Jake's game expand to include his favorite teddy bear and his grandmother. There was still affection there! The police officer had to be mistaken. There had to be another explanation, one she just couldn't think of? How could Fletcher possibly have left her and taken their son from her? What was she going to tell her mother? Her friends?

An insidious voice inside Charlotte showed her a picture of what this coming Christmas might be—no need for brightly colored presents as there would be no small child to appreciate them. Of course, her mother would be there with her, but without Jake what would be the point? Charlotte gently let go of the fire truck but left all the other toys where they lay, unwilling to open herself to the memories of their last use, unable to accept that Jake might be lost to her.

She entered her bedroom and cried until exhaustion overtook her.

Chapter 5

When your mother asks, "Do you want a piece of advice?" it is a mere formality. It doesn't matter if you answer yes or no. You're going to get it anyway.

—Erma Bombeck

The banging on the door matched the banging in Charlotte's head. Begrudegdly she left the safety of her bedroom, past clothing she didn't remember wearing and scraps of food she didn't remember eating, toward the front door.

"Charlotte? Charlotte? Honey, it's your mom. I know you are in there. Answer the door Charlotte!"

Her entire body feeling as if it was made of rubber, Charlotte barely flipped the lock on the door—an action that her mother took as sign of invitation, flinging the door open and scanning both the house and Charlotte.

Charlotte realized that she was still in her pajamas and bathrobe, though the brightness and heat radiating from the front stoop told her that it must be past midway in the outside world.

"Oh, Charlotte, Mom's here now. You don't need to worry, Mom is going to take care of you. The police are going to find Jake, and when they do, I am going to make sure that that jerk really disappears." Charlotte had finally managed to call her mother in an emotionally draining process. She did not believe that much of her side of the conversation could be considered as being spoken in English, but enough of the story must have gotten through. Her mom seemed entirely well equipped to suggest all sorts of punishments for Fletcher.

"Mom, I don't know what to do! I still don't believe it."

"You are going to start by getting yourself cleaned up. While you do that, I am going to clean up this mess." As she said this, Charlotte's mother led her back toward the bedroom and her bathroom.

When Charlotte emerged, her mother was already hard at work, and the house began to take on some semblance of normalcy; only then had Charlotte realized that her life may never be normal again as she knew it and immediately began sobbing once again. Her mother immediately halted what she was doing, rushing over in an attempt to comfort her.

"Honey, they are going to find him. I know they will."

"The police officer said I needed to find a private investigator."

"Then you need to go out and do that. You probably need to meet with a lawyer too. One of my work friends knows of a great divorce attorney. I can get you her name. I'll take care of everything here. You have your cell phone. I'll give you a call the minute I hear anything. Anything at all! I'm not going anywhere!"

"Mom, I still don't know for sure that Fletcher left me, it could be some other reason."

"Humph, we'll see. At least do what the officer said and find an investigator."

"But Mom, if you are here, what are you going to do about your work?"

"I've got time saved up. My work knows. I told them this morning that I need to be here. How about you? Have you told your work what is going on?" If Charlotte had been fully in control of her state of mind, she might have been somewhat concerned about her mother's statement as her mother had hinted that her office was looking to force employees of a certain age into early retirement, whether they were prepared for it or not. And, Charlotte, under normal circumstances, would have grown nervous about her mother giving her employer any excuse to make do without her.

"All I've told Richard is that I have a family emergency. He's really not happy with me, but I don't really care at the moment."

"How many days can you afford to stay away?"

"I have to check with him tomorrow."

"Well then, all the more reason for you to go out today."

Charlotte hated the thought of leaving the house, both in need of the phone to ring, and yet going crazy in its silence. As much as she loathed admitting it, she really did need to get out of the house. Clinging to a life raft of optimism, she suggested, "Maybe they'll come home the minute I leave the driveway?"

"I suppose it could happen. I'll let you know if they do. Now go!" Glancing back, Charlotte could see as she exited out toward her car that her mother had already begun to make herself comfortable in her home, her head hidden as she searched for cleaning products under the sink. Further debate would be futile.

<hr>

After the low balance statement from the ATM just a few days before, Charlotte wasn't sure what available funds might be at her disposal that could go toward an investigation. She assumed it was not going to be cheap. She knew that if she asked, her mother would contribute, but pride kept her quiet from asking for more help. Charlotte knew that she probably could get quite a bit of her own investigative work done at home, in front of her computer using only the internet, but her mother might notice and might start asking questions as to why a professional wasn't involved. She was going to have to do a degree of legwork the old fashioned way.

Charlotte decided to go to the bank first. She assumed that if Fletcher was attempting to disappear, he wouldn't use the debit card for their joint checking account; but in this case she did not want to assume anything, and ruling out the obvious seemed to be a logical first step.

Shortly after Fletcher had gone into business for himself, he had transferred all of their money, both personal and business accounts, to a small local bank. At the time, he had explained to her that he was doing this as the larger banks were hesitant to loan money to start-ups such as himself, and that he liked this bank because they provided each of their customers with "personal bankers" at desks rather than impersonal tellers protected from the customers, behind a large wall masquerading as a desk. Charlotte had never really seen the benefit in the arrangement as most of her transactions were either electronically conducted via direct deposit, ATM, or debit card, but in this instance, she took comfort in knowing that the person seated on the other side of the desk actually did know her husband personally and might be able to spot irregularities that could give her some clue as to his and Jake's whereabouts.

"Ah, you must be Mrs. Row! How good to finally have a chance to meet you! I must say you have an adorable son. I just love seeing his pictures when Fletcher comes in. How can I help you?" Charlotte grimaced when she realized that *their* personal banker was an absolutely stunning woman. She was immaculately dressed in a red dress that looked to be tailored perfectly to her very apparent curves. Her blonde hair had just the perfect degree of volume and bounce, and the jewelry adorning her neck and ears positively sparkled. Charlotte, with her baggy red-rimmed eyes, more-frizzed-out than-normal hair, wearing an outfit she had purchased close to a decade ago, immediately felt insignificant and realized that here, here was the woman she had seen in her paranoid vision from the other day.

Charlotte immediately changed her mind about sharing the finer details about why she wanted to review her husband's recent transactions.

"Um, yes, nice to meet you too. Err, Fletcher may have left his wallet out recently and we'd like to make sure that no one gained access to our accounts, and I, ah, just wanted to see if you might be able to review our accounts to see if there was any sort of, umm, suspicious activity on them?"

"Did you know that you can review your accounts online? I am happy to help you, of course, but I just wanted to make sure you are aware of the option. It could save you a trip."

"Yes, I normally would do that, but I really just wanted to have a second pair of eyes."

"Oh, is Fletcher traveling again?"

"Yes."

The woman began typing away on her computer. "Would you like me to review all of your accounts—the joint checking, Fletcher's account, and the business account?"

Charlotte attempted to hide her quick intake of breath, raising her hand to her face as if covering a yawn. She was only aware of the joint account and the business account.

"Yes, if you don't mind. He's not sure when he might be back to check on them himself."

"Not a problem."

The banker's fingers flew across the keyboard. "Well, I don't see any suspicious activity on any of the accounts. I had been trying to reach Fletcher about an overdraft on the business account, but it appears he took care of that before the weekend."

"And nothing on the other accounts? No out of state or large transactions?"

"Nothing that I notice as out of place. Okay, I really shouldn't be doing this because it doesn't look like you are set up as a signatory on Fletcher's secondary account, so I won't be able to print this out, but here, you are welcome to look." She turned the screen toward Charlotte. She scrolled through the list and had to agree with the banker's assessment of the legitimacy of transactions contained within the third account. Of course, that she didn't know about the existence of Fletcher's separate account made everything in it appear suspicious. She noted that there had been a number of small dollar transfers between their joint account and his business account. Additionally, there had been a number of large recurring payments to a person or company from the previously unknown third account.

Charlotte did not recognize the recipient of those payments. At least she was fairly certain she did not recognize him, her, it, or them as several of the words were abbreviated so heavily that Charlotte couldn't be sure. The last transaction had been on Friday morning, with no other clue as to where he might have gone. She was going to need to visit Fletcher's office in person to further review his records. Unfortunately, due to her late start this afternoon, she couldn't be sure that there would still be an employee in the office to let her in. Fletcher's receptionist only worked part-time. She would need to go home and find Fletcher's key, assuming that he didn't take it with him.

Charlotte attempted to memorize the name on the record, hopeful that she might see something later that would trip her memory, but was afraid that was going to be a lost cause due to the number of jumbled letters, "No, I don't see anything other than my beach trip expenses. It looks like we may have dodged a bullet."

"That's great news. Did you know that we also offer an identify protection program? Here's a pamphlet on it."

Charlotte thanked the woman for her assistance. The woman began to ask a few last-minute questions about the health and well-being of her son, and Charlotte raced out of the building as fast as she could short of running, unable to maintain the false upbeat attitude required by further small talk.

Charlotte entered her home only to discover that nearly everything within it was different than when she had left. She noticed immediately that the couch had been relocated to the center of the room and that the toys were no longer circling the den's parameter. All the floors were cleaned, and the kitchen sparkled; Charlotte noticed that even the baseboards had been wiped down. This could only mean that her mother was settling in as a guest for the long haul. Remembering back to when Jake was first born and her mother had acted similarly, Charlotte opened the pantry doors. As she thought, there were items on the shelves that she knew she had not bought, and those items which had been purchased by her had been shuffled in some mysterious methodology that she had never quite cracked. At least when her sister organized her pantry, everything was sorted alphabetically by food group and then by height.

Her mother entered the kitchen. "Back already? Did you find a good one?"

"Er, I decided to do a little up-front work myself."

"Charlotte, you know that I am glad to help you with the money to hire someone."

"I know, Mom. Any update?"

"No, sweetie. Everything has been quiet here."

"I am going to look for Fletcher's office key. Maybe he left a note, appointment book entry, or something else his staff missed."

"Charlotte, I do think you are better off calling a professional."

"Mom, this is something I need to do. Besides, I have to make sure it's still business as usual over there. We still don't know that he just hasn't been in an accident. What if he wakes up from a coma and everything he has worked for over the last few years is gone? I can't do that to us." When she originally started making this argument, Charlotte had intended just to get around her mother's suggestion; only after she said it did she realize that she actually meant it. She needed to maintain her faith that his absence was not intentional, that she would see their son again, and that they still had a future together. She might not be able to control the when of her husband's and son's return, and she might be an emotional wreck right now, but perhaps there were things, like his business, that she could control, at least temporarily.

"I think you need to be more concerned about yourself and getting Jake back."

"I am, Mom. I just need to do this."

"If it's about the money . . ."

"It's not just about the money, Mom."

"Well, can I at least make you something to eat?"

"I'm really not that hungry, Mom."

"Nonsense. I'll make you a sandwich." Her mother busied about the room, ignoring all further objections.

"How do you like the changes I made to the den?"

"I noticed that you moved the couch."

"Barb recently got back from Shanghai. You remember Barb, don't you? Her husband has started consulting and now goes overseas to give presentations to companies all over the world. She gets to travel along but has to keep herself occupied while he is working. This last time, she decided to take a class on the fundamentals of feng shui and was telling me all about how to place furniture in the room. I figure you could use all the positive qi you could get. I hope you don't mind." Charlotte's mother continued to talk about the potential benefits of opening up the room's polarity and how the degree of clutter that Charlotte had allowed to enter into her dwelling was stifling the positive energy.

"I know you think you can find everything, but really, I found toys everywhere. Did you know I even found one of Jake's trucks in the freezer? This way is so much better. I really think you are going to be able to feel the difference by the time you come back tomorrow. I'll have finished fixing the den, and I will move on to the bedrooms."

"Mom, really, you don't have to do any of this. I can take care of myself."

"Can you, honey? Can you? No, I saw you this afternoon. I think it is best if I stay for a while. Luckily, I brought my bag. I've already brought it in from the car. You can go to his office if that is what you think you have to do, but I am going to go put out flyers."

Charlotte felt every jab from her mother's attempt at a guilt trip, but her mother's efforts had only stubbornly cemented her decision to continue her investigation her way. She searched through Fletcher's drawers and scanned the nightstand. Unfortunately, the office key was not to be found. She would have no choice but wait until the following day, which meant that she was going to have to update Richard as to what was going on if she wanted to ensure that she also still had a job to return to.

Chapter 6

*They usually have two tellers in my local bank, except
when it's very busy, when they have one.*

—Rita Rudner

The alarm clock blared. Another day had begun without
Jake's morning assault. Charlotte took calming breaths to fight
off the impending panic attack. She remained committed to her
plan from the evening before. She was going to find out what
that separate account was for and who was getting paid. She
was going to find a clue as to what might have happened to her
family. She was a good mother. Fletcher could not have done
this to her. She was going to find them. She was going to keep
their future intact.

Charlotte entered her office building having decided that
it would be better to explain what was going on to Richard
face-to-face rather than attempt to do so over the phone.
After her experience telling her mother, she didn't know how

coherent she would have sounded if she attempted another conversation about it surrounded by her semi-empty house. When she left, true to her word, her mother had darted into her bedroom to begin realigning that room as well.

"Richard, I need to talk you. Can we go to your office?"

"I don't have much time. Are you aware of the burden your absence has placed on the rest of the staff?"

"I know, but I really need to talk you."

"Fine. Let's go to my office."

Richard shut the door as they entered his office, Charlotte nervously sitting down in the companion chair at his desk. Richard did not sit down.

"Now tell me, what has been going on that has kept you away?"

Charlotte explained coming home to the empty house, the missing clothes, the missing person's report, and her desire to continue with her investigation. As she told her story, Richard stuck out his lips and began to nod his head as if Charlotte was confirming something long suspected.

"Charlotte, you know we have a generous paid time off policy." Richard's statement was true, the firm did offer a healthy amount of time off, except that very rarely did anyone ever use it as extended absences were universally frowned upon. He began to pace around the room as he spoke. "And you've been with us for what, five, six years now?" It was closer to eight. "You should know that you don't need to make up stories to explain needing some time off now and then. I expect these sorts of things from the interns, but you should be more mature than that."

"Richard, I truly, truly wish I was making this up. An amber alert was issued. Did you not see it?"

"I don't have time to watch television. The police haven't any leads?"

"None that I am aware of. They haven't even checked in with me."

Richard grumbled to himself. "Charlotte, given your length of service to the company, I am willing to extend a degree of patience while you work out whatever is going on with your home life. I meant what I said before. I need a team who is dedicated and focused on the client as soon as they pass through our doors. I will hold your position for you while you attend to family matters, but I cannot do so indefinitely. I will need you to check in with me regularly and understand that we may have to make a change if your absence begins to cause a burden on the firm." Richard's forehead had begun to bead with sweat, whether from the exertion of disciplining Charlotte or being forced to extend to her a degree of consideration. Charlotte couldn't be sure.

"I understand."

"And you also recognize that anytime you take beyond what vacation time you have already stored up will be unpaid."

"Yes, I know."

"And, Charlotte." Richard's mustache swished like an irritated walrus.

"Yes, Richard?"

"Find some eyedrops. You look awful."

As she exited Richard's office, she felt, not happy under any circumstances, but at least proud that she had been able to keep a cool head about her. A part of her remained disappointed that Richard could suggest that she would come up with such as story on a whim, but Richard was one of those aging individuals who saw every one of the younger generations in a negative light. The number of times Richard had made casual references to her age had led Charlotte to believe that he did not consider her one of the upstart entitled kids; in fact, she had been under the impression that he believed she was older than she actually was, but his comments today proved otherwise. Then again, Richard had never really been supportive of anyone.

She gathered her things and returned to her parked car. The interior was an oven, having been left out in the sun. The engine refused to crank.

"Great. Just great!" She tried the key again. The car finally started up on the fourth try. Charlotte hoped that it was just the older car's way of responding to the hot day and not indicative of something more expense that would need to be attended to. She made a mental note to park in the shade at Fletcher's office.

"I should have asked to borrow his car on Friday." With his need to travel, Fletcher made a point to ensure that his vehicle's maintenance was always up to date. Occasionally, Charlotte would borrow his car when she knew she was going to drive several miles out of the city as it tended to be more reliable, but in this case, she had been so eager to go on her trip that she hadn't even thought to bring up the question.

The remainder of the drive between her office and Fletcher's passed without event. The backmost corner of the parking lot surrounding the office park did still remain in the shade, and although it wouldn't last the whole day, Charlotte hoped that it might offer enough protection to avoid another repeat performance.

She entered Fletcher's office and was greeted by his receptionist, a woman approaching middle age, but waging an unwinnable campaign against it. Her appearance consisted of a highly liberal use of at-home hair dye, heavy liquid eyeliner, and clothes that were most likely designed for someone at least one, if not two, generations younger. Those same clothes were stretched to the maximum that could be considered to be business appropriate as she was positively a tank. Charlotte realized that she could not place the woman's name. At some point during the last few years, she had stopped entering the building on those rare occasions that she needed to swing by, barely needing to turn off the car when she did, as her husband would meet her in the parking lot up front. Additionally, Fletcher had told her about a turnover in the position. Charlotte hadn't felt it necessary to keep up with his staff's comings and goings, something she regretted now.

"Oh, Charlotte, I am so glad you've come in. We haven't heard from Fletcher in quite some time. It is not like him at all. Is he okay?"

Charlotte did not quite know how exactly to answer this question. She worried that if she told the entire story, his staff might leave, and while Richard had given her some time to get things in order, she knew deep down that she wouldn't be given the opportunity to find replacements. If she was honest with herself, she really didn't know what exactly his staff did, and so would not be able to train any replacements she could find, especially if all the staff left at once. At the same time, they might be able to help her piece together where Fletcher and Jake might have gone or at least provide some other ideas as to where she should look for clues. She needed them on her side.

Charlotte settled on avoiding the question. "I'm going to need to grab some things from Fletcher's office."

Luckily, the phone saved Charlotte from further explanation. She stood around just long enough for the receptionist to answer the call and ensure it was not Fletcher calling in before launching herself toward the back of the office, walking purposefully as if her being there was an everyday occurrence and not noteworthy at all.

A few inspirational posters hung from the wall. Charlotte remembered back to when she and Fletcher had ordered them. Fletcher had been out of the regular workforce for close to a month. He had gone on a few interviews with companies cut from the same cloth as his previous employer and attended a number of job fairs. It was at one of those job fairs that he had received a copy of a book on entrepreneurship and wealth creation that had changed their lives. Suddenly, he was no longer content to merely reenter the workplace as an employee.

He had completed his reading in less than a week, a previously unheard of pace for him, and had surprised Charlotte at her work with flowers, the envy of her coworkers for several days. Fletcher had taken her out to the restaurant where they had had their first date, and over wine and nearly to-die-for steak, they had discussed his dream for a better future, a future where they had the control.

"Charlotte, you should have seen the other people in that room. No one wanted to be there. There was just no way that there were enough jobs available to support the attendance, and you could tell from everyone's eyes that they recognized it too. How is someone who has been working twice as long as me going to be able to compete with someone fresh out of school? And if they do get a job, what is the chance that the company isn't going to turn around and downsize them in a few months? What if we were to launch our own business? We could run it as we saw fit, and maybe if we are successful, give some of those people a second chance."

"What would we do?"

"Have you come across the term SaaS?"

"No."

"It stands for Software as a Service, and I think it is going to be the next big thing. It will take a bit of our savings to start up, but just imagine it—we could potentially be the next Google!" He continued on passionately explaining all the benefits companies might see by using software hosted and managed by a third party. After the dinner, flush from promoting his dream, Charlotte and Fletcher had barely made it into the house before they were upon each other, clothing draping the couch, floors—anything but their bodies.

Charlotte caught herself smiling at the memory. After an evening, or what could be considered an early, early morning, of celebratory debauchery, they had ordered the posters to help keep Fletcher motivated while programming. They both viewed the messages as hokey, and they at first had only framed and hung them as a joke, but Fletcher had told her that their physical presence made the whole idea seem more real. It was their first business investment.

When they had come up with this idea, the cell phone of choice by the business professionals was the Blackberry. Fletcher's original idea centered on a PC-based website. Of course, the iPhone was released shortly after turning the smartphone world on its head. Soon everyone was developing apps and cloud solutions. Fletcher's whole product had to be redeveloped for mobile phone use. This was one of a number of start-up snags, and it soon became even more critical that Charlotte continue at her current position for health benefits in addition to the regular salary as she soon learned that Jake was on his way.

Charlotte entered Fletcher's office and closed the door. The room was sparsely decorated by a few clippings from his original business debut: a pair of framed photographs, a small one of her taken during their honeymoon, and a much larger shot of Jake. The desk surface itself was fairly empty aside from a miniature scanner, a container of pens, and the computer. Unlike her work, Fletcher was able to run a fairly paperless business. Charlotte was momentarily thankful that Fletcher did so much of his work via his cell phone, and as such, rarely removed the computer from its docking station as she realized that the office would definitely have been a dead end if his laptop had also been missing.

She awoke the computer from its hibernation mode and accessed Fletcher's digital appointment book software. There were a number of appointments on the calendar for this week, all of which were within an hour or less drive from the office. She additionally noted that he had blocked out the entire weekend as a personal appointment but did not provide any additional details. Charlotte scrolled back to Friday and saw in the calendar his last appointment was with a Peter Demsey.

Fletcher not only sold cloud-based software services, he used them as well, and Charlotte was able to find the name within Fletcher's contacts and dialed the number.

"Demsey Law Office," the voice answered.

Her heart began to plummet once again, reminded of her mother's recommendation that she find a divorce lawyer. She considered the possibility that her husband might have already found one. "Uh, yes, umm, this is probably highly unusual, but my name is Charlotte Row, and I am calling about my husband, Fletcher Row."

"Yes, hello, Mrs. Row. What can I help you with?"

"Did you meet with my husband on Friday?"

"Yes, I did."

"Are you . . . are you a divorce lawyer?"

"No, Mrs. Row, I am your husband's corporate legal representative. Why do you ask? You aren't seeking one, are you?"

Charlotte closed her eyes and exhaled the breath she didn't realize she was holding. She began yet another retelling of the events leading up to today. While it certainly wasn't getting any easier in the telling, this being her third time, she was becoming more adept at sticking to the highlights and less likely to burst into a sob fest.

After she was done, there was a long pause on the other end of the line.

"Charlotte, may I call you Charlotte?" He asked. She affirmed.

"I've been working with your husband for the last several weeks, refining some of the details of his business growth plan, and I can tell you that while I have counseled him to start preparing a key man policy, to my knowledge he had not yet set that up, neither am I aware of any sort of succession plan."

"What does that mean exactly?"

"I am afraid that it means that unless he had set up another form of savings, he has not yet set up an insurance plan which would allow you to offer a financial incentive for bringing on someone else to run the business for you. Additionally, he has not given signature rights to any of his existing employees, which means that you can step in and take over if you want, which, I would caution you, will require a significant portion of your time. Taking over would be your right as his spouse, but as you've said, you don't know if or when he might be returning.

You also do have the option of selling the company outright if he doesn't return, but as Fletcher's business was his software product, I am not sure how valuable the business would look to others without Fletcher behind it. I need you to recognize that before you take over full-time or find a trustworthy person to help you—the company is essentially dead without Fletcher."

"And he didn't say anything about leaving or an emergency when you met with him on Friday?"

"No. Nothing at all."

"I see."

"Charlotte, there are others out there that can help you with the valuation of the company if you choose to attempt to sell it. I am happy to refer you to one of them if you'd like."

Charlotte briefly wondered if Fletcher could have been setting up a separate slush savings fund as Peter had mentioned, and if that was what the mysterious third account was for, though was not too optimistic about it as she has seen more debits than credits in her review of the transactions. She decided that she was going to need to continue to dig around Fletcher's computer to see if there might be any other leads.

Fully in research mode, Charlotte was nearly startled out of her chair, her heart leaping, when she heard a voice say,

"Oh good, Fletch, you're back."

Chapter 7

Don't go around saying the world owes you a living.
The world owes you nothing. It was here first.

—Mark Twain

"Oh, I'm sorry, I heard typing in here and assumed it was Fletcher." A tall, lean yet muscular man with a dark complexion stood in the doorway. It was Daniel, Fletcher's newest employee. Charlotte tried to keep her disappointment from crushing her.

"Hi, Daniel, you're Okay. I was just looking around Fletcher's desk for . . ." Charlotte's mind went blank. She couldn't think of a cover story, and based on the conversation with the lawyer just a few seconds ago, she was most likely going to need to solicit help keeping Fletcher's business afloat while she continued her investigation.

"Daniel, Fletcher and Jake have been missing since Friday," she began. She even told Daniel about the police officer's suspicion that this was a case of parental child abduction, burying her head in her hands while waiting for Daniel to pass judgment on her family situation. It took several minutes for Daniel to speak.

"Charlotte, Fletcher doesn't strike me as someone who gives up." Charlotte looked up. "Let me tell you about myself. I never knew my father. My mother was an addict and kept my sister and I around just long enough to ensure that her government check came in. When she had her money, she would force us out, and we spent most of our childhood in various shelters, always coming to collect us ahead of the next check-up. After a particularly long period in the shelters, we finally learned that she wasn't going to be coming for us. She'd OD'd. I swore that neither my sister nor I would be like her. I was nearly sixteen, so I got myself a fake ID to add a few years on so that I would be considered an *adult*," and he nearly sneered while he said the word, "so that I could get a job. It wasn't great work, but it allowed me to feed us while my sister while finished school. She enlisted after she graduated, and is going to be enrolling in college after this tour." Daniel beamed with pride when spoke about his sister.

"Unfortunately, one day, when I was nineteen, I passed a convenience store while coming home from work. It seems that someone had just attempted to purchase alcohol with a fake ID, and when the cashier called him on it, some other kids had rushed in, assaulted the cashier, and robbed the place. The police saw me walking down the street, pulled me in for questioning, and found the fake ID which I forgotten I still had in my wallet. I did make the most of my time as a guest of the state and earned my GED."

"I am telling you this because I've never lied on job applications about my background, and I know that I am not exactly what most consider a highly desirable candidate, but Fletcher listened to my story. I was wearing my best clothes, which wasn't saying much at the time, but he didn't see the stains. He saw me. And he's given me a chance."

"I've seen a lot of runners in my life. I've seen a lot of people looking to blame their problems on others while looking for handouts. Fletcher's not one of those people. I will say, though, that he perhaps takes too many chances with people."

"What do you mean?" asked Charlotte, her eyebrows knitting together in confusion.

"What I mean is that I'm grateful that he took a chance with me, but I do know that he sometimes makes decisions with his heart and not his head. Some people might see that as a weakness to exploit in others."

The receptionist peeked into the room. "Sorry to interrupt, but I have Avnex Corporation on the line, and they need to speak to you, Daniel."

Daniel nodded his head at Charlotte as he stepped out of the room. "Okay, thanks, Stacey. I'm sorry, I need to take this call."

"Sure. I'll keep looking to see if I can find anything."

The receptionist smiled. "I thought you might like some coffee?" She waved a mug in hand, a bit of the liquid rising above the rim, the motion creating a drip down the side of the mug.

"Thank you, Stacey." She was mentally thanking Daniel for mentioning her name and saving Charlotte from the painful process of attempting a conversation when it is obvious the other person knows you more than you know them. It was also a nice experience for Charlotte to be on the other side of the desk for once. "I am going to be covering for Fletcher for a while, but he left before he could show me some of the basics, and it's been a while since I've been in here. I may need your help with some of the day to day work."

"Sure. Is everything Okay with him?" Stacey brought the cup over to the desk, only then noticing the trail of coffee that would result in a ring of liquid on the desk. "Sorry about that, I'll get a napkin to clean that up." Stacey returned with a napkin in hand, and as she picked the mug back up to clean up the wet circle, her hand knocked over the jar of pens, sending them across the desk and onto the floor. Stacey, forgetting about the coffee, frantically moved in to pick up the pens, which resulted in another spill. Charlotte noticed lights shining on the phone.

"That's okay, Stacey. It looks like we have calls coming in. Why don't you go back up to the front and take those? I'll clean up in here."

After Stacey departed, Charlotte called the police station for an update on their progress. The person on the other end of the line informed her in very brisk tones that a car matching the description of the make of Fletcher's had been found at a bus depot. This location had bus routes spanning across the country, and unless they could find some form of paper trail, additional lead, or currently unidentified witness, it could be the end of the line for their investigation. There was no sign of damage to the car and no evidence within which might indicate where they might be going. None of the ticket counter employees interviewed remembered passengers in particular matching the description of Jake, but the ticket could have been purchased with cash in advance.

Charlotte was unsure how to process this new development in the case. She could not think of many reasons for Fletcher to leave his car at the bus depot without purchasing a ticket other than the obvious: he not only took the bus someplace, but he also planned so far ahead that the tickets were already purchased. This would mean that he potentially was planning to leave in advance of her spontaneous beach trip. But why would he take the bus to begin with? Unless he did not want to put the miles on his car, or—and Charlotte's breath caught—he did not want anyone to be able to trace his plates.

The phone began to ring the moment Charlotte hung up with the police. Stacey was on the other end. "Sorry, Charlotte, this person is demanding to speak with you."

Chapter 8

When life is too easy for us, we must beware or we may not be ready to meet the blows which sooner or later come to everyone, rich or poor.

—Eleanor Roosevelt

"Hello, Mr. Row?"

"Mr. Row is unavailable. How can I help you?"

"I told the woman answering the phone that I had to be put immediately in contact with Mr. Row."

"As I said, he is not available at this time. I am his wife. How can I help you?"

"I see. So you are a co-owner of Archer Service Solutions?"

"I am." At least Charlotte thought she was. She actually had never seen the legal document regarding the business's incorporation, but she had to assume that she had some rights based on what the corporate lawyer had mentioned.

"Well, Mrs. Row, I am rather surprised that you are so free to admit your connection. I would have thought you might try to distance yourself more."

"I beg your pardon?" replied Charlotte, quite confused by the progression of this conversation.

"If you have an ownership stake in the company, you of course are aware of the illegal actions your company has been taking?"

"What?"

"Now, Mrs. Row, it's well documented that willful ignorance is not an excuse."

"I am afraid I don't know what you are talking about."

"I am talking about the fact that Archer Service Solutions is willfully and consciously promoting a product that is in violation of my client's patents!"

As Charlotte knew well, the business of patent litigation was still booming even in the current economy, and as a result, a new class of patent lawyer was coming to prominence. Those outside of the industry referred to them in disgust as patent trolls. These individuals would work with partners who would register for frivolous patents with the hopes that they might one day find an excuse to yell infringement. Large, too big to fail organizations would dole out sums to settle, not because the case had merit, but just because it was cheaper to remove the gnats that way. However, not satisfied, these same trolls could easily turn around and bankrupt emerging technology companies with shallower pockets through litigation, even if the courts found there to be no case of infringement.

"Sir, my husband's product in no way copies an existing service."

"I have papers on my desk, coming directly from your organization, that explicitly suggest otherwise."

"I don't know what papers you are referring to."

"Oh, you will. Now my client, who has every right to shut you down, is willing to consider a solution which would allow you to keep your doors open, provided certain modifications are made to your program and you agree to an ongoing royalty, in addition to a one-time settlement for past damages. He thinks that a degree of competition is healthy for everyone. You will be receiving a cease-and-desist letter from my firm later today, in addition to our terms for settlement. I would encourage you to make Mr. Row aware of this matter immediately. Good day."

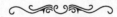

Immediately following the call, Charlotte had dug into Fletcher's computer files. The odious man on the other end of the line had never identified himself or his client, so Charlotte was still as clueless about this latest threat as she was about her family's whereabouts—and even less interested. Charlotte paused to wonder if Fletcher might have regularly received calls like that and silently felt somewhat ashamed to be part of the industry, even though she believed her firm was above that sort of practice.

While she hadn't yet found the smoking gun that would explain the existence of Fletcher's separate savings account, she had gained access to his e-mail. Within it, she was able to see a troubling e-mail conversation chain of e-mails. She scrolled to the bottom and read upward.

Date: June 15th
From: Marshall Thomas
To: Fletcher Row

I need my money. I will be at your office to pick up my check.

To: Marshall Thomas

Marshall. You didn't complete the work. I'm not going to pay for work what isn't complete.

To: Fletcher Row

What do you mean you aren't going to pay? I put in my hours!

To: Marshall Thomas

I don't know and don't care how many hours you put in. I have nothing to show for it. I certainly can't charge my customers based on what I've received from you.

To: Fletcher Row

You just want to cheat me. You think that just because you are some big boss now that you can get away with not paying people like me.

To: Marshall Thomas

I'm not going to discuss this further with you.

To: Fletcher Row

Listen, I need my money. You don't want to mess with me. I'll come to your office to pick it up.

To: Marshall Thomas

I am not going to write you a check. If you come to my office, I will have the police come and escort you out.

She left Fletcher's office to see if she could catch Daniel before he departed for another day of sales calls.

"Daniel, are you familiar with someone called Marshall Thomas?"

"Yeah, sure. He was a subcontractor Fletch has considering using."

"Did he come into the office recently to ask about a check?"

"I heard about that. It was a couple of weeks ago. I was told that he basically sat in the office until Fletcher had to call the police on him."

"So Fletcher was there?"

"No, actually he was out making sales calls at the time, but Regan and Stacey were there."

"I'm not sure who Regan is."

"Oh yeah, Regan is Inside Sales for us."

"Is she part-time?" Charlotte looked around—the only people in the small office that she had seen were Stacey and Daniel.

"Well, yes, the job was part-time. But Fletcher was going to let her go last week. I assume he did that while Stacey and I were out of the office." As soon as he mentioned this, Charlotte realized that he vaguely mentioned someone named Regan not too long ago.

"Why did he let her go?"

"He didn't tell me anything, but I can only guess he got sick of her drama. That lady was always getting worked up about something. We wouldn't see her for a day or so, but then she'd walk back in here like she hadn't just made all of us cover for her. I guess she knew how to work all the angles though; on her good days, she could get us an appointment anywhere. Speaking of which, I need to head out for some calls which will probably take up the rest of the day. I guess I'll turn in my expenses to you then?"

"I guess so." Charlotte briefly considered mentioning the cease-and-desist letter. It hadn't arrived yet, and all she had seen thus far were expenses. "Good luck."

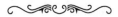

"Charlotte. Mr. Peace is here to see you."

"I'm not sure who that is Stacey. Did Fletcher expect him?"

"It's on his calendar; it's his monthly appointment with the accountant."

"Oh, I guess send him back." Charlotte, back in Fletcher's office, smoothed the errant hairs that she could feel sticking out in every direction. She thought to herself that this meeting could prove very beneficial as the accountant might be able to shed light on the mystery account. She also hoped that he might be able to paint a better picture of the health of the company, though she suspected she already knew what he was going to say.

"Hi, Mrs. Row. Good to meet you. I've heard all about you from Fletcher." When had she stopped asking Fletcher for details about his workday? Here was yet another example of someone who knew her better than she knew them. The man before her was most likely in his later forties or earlier fifties, with just the smallest hint of gray hair, giving him an instant credible and distinguished look about him. He was dressed smartly without looking out of place in his business suit—a business suit that stated to the observer that it was designed for comfort and wearability, rather than merely serving as a means for a designer to slap its name on another article of clothing.

"Hi, Mr. Peace. Umm, I am afraid you have an advantage over me at the moment. I'm trying my best to get my hands wrapped around Fletcher's day to day here, but I am not prepared at all for this meeting."

"Oh?"

"Yes, um, maybe you can give me a rough overview and we can take it from there?"

"Of course, not a problem. First, I should clarify. Yes, I am a certified public accountant, but I'm an independent corporate financial consultant, not just a bookkeeper. May I drive on Fletcher's computer?"

Charlotte nodded in affirmation and gestured that Mr. Peace could have a seat. She stood behind him so that she might be able to see where he was navigating in order for her to repeat the process if she had to on her own. A series of rapid keystrokes later, Mr. Peace had opened up a financial reporting package and printed out a series of reports for them to review.

"How familiar are you with the business model?" asked Mr. Peace. Charlotte shrugged.

"Well, as Fletcher explained it to me, the business model has three separate forms of income. Customers are asked to pay an annual fee when they first sign up, as well as purchase a package of licenses depending on the number of users they anticipate. The customers then use the product to manage a menu of available services provided by partners who pay a monthly fee in order to be included in the product's database. Now obviously, if customers aren't purchasing a particular service, then there is no value to the subcontractor and they stop using the service, which means that even if one customer grows in the number of users—unless they use a variety of services—that customer could consume a number of resources and cost the company money from lost subscribers. Lost subs of course mean there are fewer services that can be offered to potential new customers. The third source of income is the service purchased itself. Your company receives a fixed commission for services managed through the tool. Does this all make sense to you?"

Once again, Charlotte nodded her head. She at least had paid attention to this much when Fletcher was first preaching about the potential brightness of their future together.

"Good. Now unfortunately, as you can see here," said Mr. Peace while pointing at a section of the report, "the last few months have seen a drop in subscribers. This may or may not be related to a similar drop in the marketing expenses. It could also have something to do with the quality of the servers. I'm not an expert, but I believe those are probably out of date by this point. I know that Fletcher just started to increase his salary within the last quarter." This was news to Charlotte as she had seen no such adjustment to their checking account and attempted to hide the surprise, hurt, and anger from her face so that Mr. Peace would not become sidetracked from his report. "But based on my month to month projections, the company really is going to need an injection of cash in order to make the necessary upgrades it needs to maintain the existing subscriber base. Obviously, without that base, you will lose customers and will be forced to close your doors, so it is a rather critical investment. I mentioned this to Fletcher last month. Did you and he talk about what you wanted to do?"

"We did not." Charlotte nearly spat out. She was beginning to understand why Fletcher may have run away, but she still couldn't believe that he wouldn't have at least mentioned how bad things were going—not even once. "How much is needed?"

"Well, luckily, memory is cheaper now than it was when Fletcher launched, and you might be able to outsource the servers, so I'd recommend $10,000."

Chapter 9

There is no despair so absolute as that which comes
with the first moments of our first great sorrow, when
we have not yet known what it is to have suffered and
be healed, to have despaired and have recovered hope.

—George Eliot

Their savings account certainly did not include $10,000 in slush money. After Mr. Peace—or Frank, as he informed her while she sat there in stunned sticker shock—left, Stacey had come into the office to inform her in a panic that one of her sons was in jeopardy of expulsion from school, and that she had to leave immediately to attend to him. With Daniel still on sales calls, there was no one left at the office to answer the phone. It didn't ring often, which was either lucky or not so lucky depending on how Charlotte chose to consider it, but it did interrupt her continued dive into Fletcher's e-mails and hard drive.

Unfortunately, she was unable to find a file that listed all of Fletcher's passwords and so was unable to access the mystery bank account further. She had been hoping that she might be able to cross-reference the transactions with either his address book or his appointment calendar. And while she saw a few other unpleasant e-mails, she wasn't able to find anything else that might suggest where he had gone, such as a travel brochure or booking confirmation. "I bet he has a private e-mail address too," thought Charlotte.

Charlotte navigated to free e-mail sites and typed through the alphabet in the log-in screen, hoping that Fletcher would have turned on an auto-complete function on his computer. If he had set up a secondary personal e-mail address, he had done so with care as there were no results.

It was well after the end of the business day when Charlotte finally turned the lights off in Fletcher's office. She left the building deflated. "I don't know what I thought I thought I might be able to find in there." All she had been able to find was more debt and no leads. The sky was beginning to darken; and as she drove home, she was overwhelmed by missing Jake, not knowing what to think about Fletcher, and definitely feeling over her head, left with the problems from his business.

When she entered her house, she immediately heard the dishwasher running. Her mom had continued to be busy while she had been out. The only clutter, if you could call it that, was a neat stack of today's mail placed next to a pile of flyers on the table. Each of these flyers contained a picture of Jake taken at Christmas at her mother's house, with her mother's cell phone number listed and a statement about a reward for information. Charlotte glanced at the pile of envelops not showing Jake's wonderful smile. The return address made it obvious that these were bills, and she left them as they were—unopened.

Charlotte walked over to the wine rack and—as all of the glasses were currently in the wash, whether they needed to be or not—pulled the cork and took a few sips while she waited for the dishwasher cycle to end. Her eyes kept being drawn to Jake's picture, and she was suddenly hit by a sense of vertigo likely caused by the alcohol hitting her empty stomach. Though she had not touched either stack of papers, the flyers seemed to retreat; Jake becoming smaller and further away while the pile of bills grew menacingly.

Charlotte tore her eyes away from the flyers, settling them back on the wine bottle. The strength she had attempted to show all day, with varying degrees of success, fled from her, leaving her exhausted, miserable, and alone. Charlotte glanced again at the dishwasher continuing to clang away. The dial on its front had barely moved. "The hell with it," Charlotte muttered aloud to herself, turning the bottle up, drinking heavily directly from the bottle. She was nearly a third of the way through the bottle—her face streaked with tears she didn't recall shedding—and had begun talking to the image of Jake on the flyer, telling him how much she missed him, when the door opened and her mother—stapler and tape strip in hand—walked back into the house.

Her mother took in the scene and, without speaking, walked back out of the door, returning moments later with Charlotte's sister in tow.

"That son of a bitch. Look what he has done to you." Charlotte's mother never cursed, and Charlotte was momentarily stunned back into the present. Her mother came over and wrapped her arms around the sobbing Charlotte. "Please tell me you haven't been like this all day."

Her sister stood slightly to the side, arms crossed. "Yes, Charlotte, what have you done today? We've been out papering the city with flyers trying to find *your* son. Mom tells me that you've been at *his* work all day. If it was me, I would let that bastard's business crumble and focus all my time on Jake. Mom tells me that you haven't even hired a real investigator yet! This is no time for some do-it-yourself shit!"

"Cecilia! That type of language is not helpful at all," their mother said, but Charlotte could tell from a watery eyed glance that her mother very much agreed with her sister and had most likely scolded her sister out of habit.

"The police think they found his car at the bus station, but they don't have any idea where they might have gone from there." Charlotte choked out while gasping for breaths between sobs.

"That bastard!" shouted her mother.

"I still don't know for certain that he actually did leave me."

"Charlotte Annabelle Mackenzie, will you listen to yourself? I did not raise my daughters to be doormats. Living in denial is not going to get your son back."

"No, Mom, it's not denial. I really don't know. I went through his work e-mail and saw a threatening message from one of his subcontractors, demanding money."

Cecilia sneered. "Let me guess, he was too broke to pay."

"His side said that the guy didn't complete the work."

"Right, I am sure he didn't. Wasn't that just convenient? When are you going to admit that he just doesn't have what it takes to make it. He obviously has realized it and left you holding the bag."

"Daniel doesn't think he is the type to run from his problems."

"Who the hell is Daniel?"

"Cecilia!"

"Sorry, Mom. Who is Daniel?"

"He is one of Fletcher's sales people."

"Charlotte dear, I am sorry, but I am just too angry to hear that name right now," cautioned her mother.

Cecilia snorted. "So some guy that you barely know is a better judge of character than your family. This same guy, who works in a profession that is paid to tell you what you want to hear, obviously couldn't be trying to manipulate you into continuing to write him a check."

Her sister had a point; Charlotte didn't know Daniel very well. He had even admitted to a criminal past, whether or not he had actually committed a crime; but she just could not accept that her husband, the same person who routinely would throw all the chips in during a poker game regardless of his hand, would back down from a challenge. But more importantly, she knew that he thought she was a good mom. Although the evidence might be stacked against him, there was Jake to consider.

"You are wrong. He told me I was a good mother. He would never intentionally keep Jake from me."

"You don't say."

"He wouldn't! He told me that he thought I was a great mom. It was actually his favorite quality about me."

"Really, Charlotte. How are you a good mom to Jake? You send him off to day care where strangers take care of him all day so that you can support that freeloader who is draining your savings dry. Mom's told me all about your problems. You are always going on about how much you need your Ladies' Nights Out. You know, I think you are actually glad that they are gone. That's why you haven't tried to get an investigator."

Cecilia's tirade was cut off by Charlotte slapping her face.

"Girls!" screamed their mother. "That is *enough*. Out, both of you!"

Cecilia rubbed her cheek as their mother continued. "Honey, Cecilia went too far, but she has a point. I am sure that he had the best of intentions when the business launched, but neither of you ever seemed to recognize that your situation changed when Jake entered the picture. If he couldn't find a work, he easily could have stayed home with Jake. I hear that there is a growing number of stay-at-home dads now. It's perfectly respectable. Barb was just telling me about how her son-in-law is going to be staying at home now that her second grandbaby is on the way." Their mother began fixing an ice bag for Cecilia, handing it to her while gently patting her on the back. "As I've repeatedly told you, if you need money to hire the investigator, it's yours. I just need to know who to write the check out to. I'll go with you to interview them if you like. Oh, and my coworker sent me the name of that divorce lawyer. Now you might not like to hear this—she's unavailable for the next two weeks, but I've gone ahead and set you up an appointment."

"You are right, Mom." Her mother sagged in relief.

"I am glad you think so. Now after your sister has a few more minutes with that ice on her cheek, we can all go back out together and finish putting these flyers up around town."

"No, Mom. I mean you are right. That's enough. I think you and Cecilia should leave my house—now."

"Honey, you can't possibly mean that. That's the wine talking. You've had a long day. Your sister and I just want Jake to come home and what's best for you. If you don't think you can manage, I can help you get ready for bed, and then we'll go back out."

"I do mean it. I am an adult, Mom. And, Cecilia, I am a good mom even if that means taking shortcuts like frozen dinners or getting help during the day from paid professionals. I think it is time for both of you to go."

"Well! We're not going to give up," huffed her mother as she grabbed the majority of the stack of flyers from the table, a few slips of paper tumbling to the ground beneath. "Cecilia, let's give your sister some time to cool off and come to her senses."

The house shook with the force of the door slamming as they departed. Charlotte sank into one of the kitchen chairs, turning up the remaining balance of the bottle of wine. Drinking a tad too fast, some of the liquid spilled out of her mouth and onto the floor, leaving blood red droplets on the image of Jake's face.

Chapter 10

I'm selfish, impatient and a little insecure. I make mistakes, I am out of control and at times hard to handle. But if you can't handle me at my worst, then you sure as hell don't deserve me at my best.

—Marilyn Monroe

Still reeling from her confrontation with her mother and sister, Charlotte decided that one good bottle deserves another and stumbled with a second open bottle in hand toward her art studio. She mixed up a number of dark tones on her palette, including dark greens that matched the glass bottle in her hand and reds to match the contents inside. While she may have begun with every intention to paint an image of a bottle to match the bottle in hand, her strokes were unrefined and smeared themselves across the canvas.

"Oh yeah! You wanna criticize me too?" said Charlotte to the offending canvas. "Well, fine! Go ahead! You have no idea.

I love that boy! And I don't need you or—" and she wagged her brush at the bottle of blue paint in the corner of the room. "I see you over there, blue. All high and mighty with your country club memberships and trips to Paris just because it's the fourth anniversary of your fifth date. I don't need you or you judging my family." She took another swig from the now nearly empty bottle. "And I tell you what. Fletcher wouldn't have left me 'cause I'm a hot momma. He told me so."

"What? What's that?" She spun nearly around to speak to the bottle of black. "Oh yes. Can't ignore the bus, can we. Always the facts with you. Always so black and white with you." She hiccupped by giggling at her own cleverness.

"Fletcher would never take Jake on a bus anywhere. Jake gets carsick just going downtown. He'd be puking all over the place if stuck in a bus. The smell of it would be enough for the bus to turn around, and there were no reports of bus delays due to excessive pukeage now, were there?"

"Remember when we tried to go to the lake for the day, and Jake got all quiet in the backseat? Remember when I turned around to check on him, and he went all Exorcist on us? Remember how Fletcher ran thirteen miles in ninety-degree heat to the closest store to get me new clothes so that Jake and I could wait with the AC running, but with doors open so that we didn't need to sit in a car with that smell?"

She giggled again and turned toward yellow. "No, that smell lasted forever! You just can't wash that sort of thing out. We tried everything—hosing out the interior, air fresheners.

We even baked cookies and put them in the car like you are supposed to do whenever you are trying to sell your house."

"I miss his cooking. Remember those Saturday mornings when he would sneak out of bed before the rest of us to get started making breakfast, and how the smell of bacon and blueberry pancakes would fill the house? Remember how that smell would wake Jake up, and how he'd sneak into our bed so that we could all eat breakfast in bed together? Now I am hungry!"

Charlotte put her brushes down, only delaying slightly to wash off the paint so as to not ruin the brushes altogether, and wove her way down the hallway. Her eyes lingered on the couch as she recalled a night just a little over six months ago. Jake had been exceptionally good that particular night. He had eaten all his dinner without fuss, and even though the weather outside was cool, they had all enjoyed making and devouring ice cream sundaes afterward. Fletcher had turned on a streaming music service, and they had jumped around the house in their own version of a dance party, no one really minding that their moves would never get them a trophy in a real dance competition.

Dancing had evolved into Fletcher picking up Jake and "flying" him around the room like a superhero; and with his trusty assistant Dad, they had rescued Mom from all bad guys. Afterward, Jake had surprised them both by announcing without prompt that he was sleepy. This proclamation, combined with the fact that he actually had cleaned his plate, was a sure sign that another growth spurt was upon them. Charlotte had stood in the doorway as Jake attempted to dress himself in his pajamas with varying degrees of success. After a few moments, he had given up, requesting her help; and Charlotte had sighed when she saw how snug the pajama pants were growing around his waist and how high above his ankles they now rested.

After teeth were brushed, they had all sat together on the floor to read Jake's favorite story for the tenth night in a row—Jake sitting in Charlotte's lap clutching Mr. Snaps, with Charlotte and Fletcher taking turns reading the pages. Once completed, they both had tucked Jake into his bed, Charlotte lingering a few more precious seconds for extra hugs and kisses.

Charlotte had joined Fletcher on the couch where they snuggled together under a blanket as they watched the television. It was getting closer to December 21, 2012, and a number of channels were doing their best to keep viewers entertained with various apocalypses and other doomsday survival programming. She and Fletcher regularly enjoyed joking about what they would do in similar circumstances, and that evening was no exception as the feature involved a plucky group of survivors from an alien-led invasion. The aliens, of course, had arrived and fired their first shot at the Lincoln Memorial as well as other highly recognizable locations around the world, precisely at midnight eastern time on the twenty-first.

After blowing the big weapons—because obviously they had the advanced planning to prepare for such an invasion by learning all of the modern forms of humanity's language and mastering all digital communications—but deciding they only needed to bring with them one-time use weaponry, the aliens had systematically hunted down the remaining humans on foot.

Luckily for humanity, one of the group's survivors conveniently happened to be a previously ridiculed expert in Native American smoke signals and was able to put all those hurt feelings aside long enough to coordinate a multi-faceted assault. The aliens were proved to be neither history buffs nor capable of noticing abnormal cloud patterns. Humanity was saved once again, only now with a better appreciation of our past. Charlotte and Fletcher had found the whole program to be in the category of "so bad it's good" and were actually sorry to see the aliens lose.

"Well, I hope you learned something." Charlotte laughed.

"Oh yes, indeed I did," replied Fletcher "I need to start brushing up on my hieroglyphics now!"

"That wouldn't do at all. Don't you remember *Ancient Aliens*, they *invented* those! Oh no, we have to come up with something they wouldn't expect. Something completely ours!"

Fletcher chuckled, rising to go to the kitchen to get a beer. "And what would that be?"

"I don't know. Something that would be noticeable to us but wouldn't look out of place at all to someone not familiar with our culture. Like a symbol or something to let people know had been there. Or that there was danger ahead without giving anything away to the people or things chasing them."

"Oh, you've given this some thought, haven't you? Obviously, you have way too much free time. You know, if you are bored, I can think of something for you to do."

Charlotte had playfully thrown a pillow at him, and their banter, which was beginning to resemble foreplay, was abruptly halted when his phone rang.

"Sorry, Char, I need to take this. This is Fletcher Row . . ." Fletcher walked off and remained between his phone and his computer the rest of the evening. She had finally called it a night and gone to bed leaving him clicking away at the keyboard in the other room.

The room swayed from side to side as Charlotte made her way to the last few feet toward the kitchen. Some part of her brain recalled that all the dishes had been occupied in the machine when she had arrived, but their cycle was now complete. Charlotte pulled out the machine drawer, her eye catching on a goblet they had received as a wedding gift from Marie and Tom—the two choosing to ignore the fine crystal requiring delicate hand washing from the registry for a more casual set that would actually be used.

Charlotte thought back to the day Fletcher opened his doors. Fletcher had spent several weeks developing the database and user interface that would be required to support his dream. Charlotte, on the other hand, had spent those same weeks fighting to stay awake after six in the evening, and each meal that she was able to keep down was a small victory. In retrospect, perhaps he hadn't needed to open a physical sales office quite so soon. But after weeks of being sequestered in the house due to lack of gainful employment and/or programming, Fletcher had seemed desperate to get back out into the real world; it was impossible not to be infected with his enthusiasm.

One evening, he had returned in triumph. He had found a location that, although several miles away, had a reasonable rent and was positioned within easy access of many of the major traffic arteries. He proudly reported that he had been able to negotiate a deal for used furnishings that would hide some of the less aesthetically pleasing aspects of the office space. He pulled out a printout of the floor plan and showed it to Charlotte, pointing to various locations on the document as he spoke.

"When I get everything installed, you will have to come see it. The receptionist will sit here. There is a door that will keep the front office separate from the back and room to make a little waiting area. We can even hang some of your art there! I am going to put my office back here, and they are going to install the cubes here and here. There is even room for another office, so eventually I will be able to bring on another sales person. The servers will be able to go into this room over here. The air conditioning isn't the best, but that room is in its own dedicated zone. Probably the previous tenants used it for something similar. And look, I'll even be able to put in a MicroFridge like we had in college over there alongside a water cooler. It's a whole office park, imagine if I could get all of them to buy into the service! We could start making money nearly immediately!"

They had taken the glasses out for a celebratory toast. Fletcher, acting in solidarity support for her, had filled both with a mixture of apple juice and tonic water as if to trick their minds into thinking they were drinking champagne.

"Just think, Char, if I can sell this, you might never have to work again. That is, if you wanted to. If you didn't want to stay home with the kid, you could come in and run the office. It would be completely your choice. We're going to be partners! Just imagine it, when the kid is in school, we'd be able to take a trip over his or her summer break anywhere around the world. We could even take your mom as a way to thank her for the help she's offered." Fletcher's eyes had positively glowed with joy.

"That would be awesome! We would be able to get our own place at the beach, and rent it out on the weekends we weren't there too!"

Fletcher and Charlotte had talked well into the night, or at least until after 10:00 p.m., which had been a late night for her at the time, exchanging ideas as to what strengths the other would bring into the business and how they might spend their eventual freedom. These discussions had led into their dreams of a bright future for their son or daughter. The work they were doing now was going to give him or her a foundation to do whatever he or she wanted, but they would make sure that he or she never acted entitled.

Although she had stubbornly refused to consider the possibility, the thought that she might never get to see Jake grow up sneaked its way through her inebriated mind. If she couldn't find him, she might never have the chance to win the presidency, take over corporate America, or discover the cure for cancer. She would never see him find his own Mrs. Right and would never have the chance to dance with him at his wedding. Never see him proudly show off his first car bought with his own money or score the winning goal. She might not even get to see him win his first spelling bee, or even send him off on the bus for his first day of school. That being only a year off, she could already see him wearing a backpack larger than half of his body waving to her as he stepped on to the bus.

Charlotte had tried so hard not to allow these thoughts to enter her consciousness, but once there, she could not rid herself of them. Her vision blurred as she let out a primal scream. The room tossed as she slammed the dishwasher door back shut, the sound of shattered glass punctuating her cries as she spun to return to her bedroom.

In her blinding and drunken sorrow, she had forgotten about her mother's rotation of the furniture. She crashed into the couch, her body crumpled along its length, her limbs flowing over onto the floor. Exhausted in every way, she remained as she lay, allowing herself to sink into blissful unconsciousness.

Chapter 11

It is during our darkest moments that we must focus to see the light.

—Aristotle Onassis

"**M**omma?"

"Momma?"

"Mommy, I'm scared!"

"Jake, what are you scared of?"

"I'm scared of the dark. It's coming to get me!"

"Honey, the dark is not coming to get you. Do you need your night light?"

"No! That's for babies! I am four years old now, you know!"

"Yes, I do know that. You are a big boy now. How about Mr. Snaps? Does Mr. Snaps need the night light on?"

"Mr. Snaps says he does."

"Is that better, Mr. Snaps?"

"Mr. Snaps says yes."

"Okay. You try to get some sleep now, okay?"

"Okay. I love you, Mommy."

"I love you too, Jake."

Charlotte opened her eyes and cursed the brightness of the day. Her head throbbed from her overindulgence from the evening before. Her limbs were sore and tingled as blood began to recirculate through them. One of her arms in particular looked bruised and creased as she must have slept with a portion of her weight upon it, but creases looked slightly excessive to Charlotte. When she had awoken, that arm had been wrapped under a throw pillow. Charlotte moved the pillow and saw something brown and furry wedged between the cushion and the side of the couch. Charlotte reached into the crevice and pulled.

She sat up. In her hand was Mr. Snaps. Charlotte could not believe that Jake had left it behind. She grasped the bear and hugged it to her face. She imagined she could smell her son and held the bear as close as she would as if he were there.

She rose from the couch and nearly collapsed as one of her legs still was partially asleep. The pins and needles feeling was sure to arrive shortly. Her voice barely broke the silence of the house, a mere whisper, as if it was just as cautious about every slight vibration it caused as the rest of her body was. "Charlotte, you cannot keep going like this. You aren't ever going to be able to take back control of your life if you can't control yourself while you are on your own."

Very, very cautiously, she made her way back to the kitchen, desperately in need of aspirin and water, still clutching Mr. Snaps like a life raft. "So, Mr. Snaps. Jake didn't happen to tell you where he was going?" Charlotte looked at the bear, not expecting a reply, but desperately wishing it would.

"No, I guess not. I bet you are just as upset as I am to be left behind."

Charlotte opened the dishwasher and saw the damage she had caused the night before. Luckily, there were only a few casualties and she was able to pull out mug. She found the pain relief pills in the cabinet, poured herself a cup of water, and carefully sipped it down while she began brewing some coffee, catching her reflection in the surface of the machine. Her image was distorted, but she could tell that her cheekbones were sharper from lack of appetite, her eyes both puffy and yet sunken.

As she waited for the coffee to brew, she found herself continuing to talk to the bear.

"Remember that family trip when we were somewhere close to an hour away from home, and Jake suddenly realized he had left you at the house? He had pitched that epic tantrum. We had tried everything to take his mind off you, but there was just no reasoning with him, and we had no choice but to double back unless we wanted a truly miserable weekend. Last year, people in China would have been able to hear him screaming for you. He must just be growing up so fast now."

The painkillers were clearly not working fast enough, and Charlotte reached into the freezer to retrieve the cold compress they kept permanently available to treat Jake's various boo-boos, both the real and the pretend ones. She intended to place it on her forehead until the medicine began working, but noticed it was not in its usual spot. She shifted several items around only to find it buried amongst the other items. Charlotte realized that her well-meaning mother's reorganization of her house must have expanded beyond the pantry this time and into her frozen food section. Her blurry eyes came into focus upon a recent copy of *Entertainment Weekly* left open to the section featuring what's happening on TV. There in the weekly line-up was a small summary of the upcoming week's creature feature/ disaster flick.

A nugget from the first day her mother arrived took root in her mind. Something so outlandish it couldn't possibly mean anything, but a thought she couldn't shake.

Her mother answered on the third ring.

"Charlotte? Are you okay? Oh, honey, I am so glad you called. I wanted to call you all morning, but after how things had gone last night, I thought you just needed some space. I absolutely hated leaving you alone like that. I've been up all night worried about you! How are you feeling this morning? Your sister and I stayed out another couple of hours putting up posters. The city is positively covered! I just know we are going to get a hit, I just know it! Someone had to have seen something! Speaking of your sister, you probably need to apologize to her too. She was just trying to tell you what you needed to hear. I'm just sorry at how she worded things. Are you okay? Do you want me to come back over? I still have my bag packed!"

"Mom, I'm not calling to apologize."

"Well, Charlotte, clearly you weren't in your right mind last night. And I know you have been under a ton of strain, but that really is no excuse for poor behavior. You owe your sister an apology. Did you realize that she delayed her vacation out west just so she could come and help out with the search? She's just in the other room, let me go get her."

"No, Mom. I'm not calling about that."

"Oh, you need the name of that attorney. Hold on, I have it somewhere in my purse."

"No, Mom!"

"The police have an update!"

"No, Mom." Charlotte sighed. "No, that would have been fantastic, but no. No further updates from them."

"Well, then," Charlotte could hear her mother's voice tightening, "if you don't have an update from the police, don't want the attorney's name, and aren't calling to apologize, I frankly can't think of what you want."

"Mom, you mentioned that when you were cleaning my house you found something in the freezer?"

"Yes, I did, one of Jake's trucks. I think it was that fire truck you gave him last Christmas, actually. You know, Charlotte, I sometimes wonder how you could find anything at all in your house."

"Mom, that's just it. I could find things. You might not have understood the method behind my madness, but there was place for everything, including Jake's toys."

"Well, I'd like to hope that the freezer is not where you keep his things. A boy needs to have access to his trucks. I'm not sure what this has to do with anything. Are you having a difficult time finding where I put things? I can come over and show you where everything is."

"Of course we don't keep his toys in the freezer."

"Well, I should hope not. The plastic would get brittle, you know, and break. And you can't afford to be throwing away toys.

"Mom, you aren't letting me talk."

"Well, what is it, Charlotte?"

"You know how I like watching the disaster flicks and the creature features on the weekends?"

"What, those B movies with the bad computer graphics?"

"Yes, those."

"Fletcher and I joked once that we would have to develop our own sort of secret code to communicate with each other if there was ever a monster invasion or an impending doom. Something that we would recognize as being out of place, but something that wouldn't trigger any alarms to someone else who wasn't as familiar with us."

"Charlotte, I really don't see how any of that is important right now."

"Mom, don't you see? That toy had absolutely no business being in the freezer! And this morning, I found Mr. Snaps wedged between the couch cushion. I thought at first that maybe Jake is just getting older and doesn't need his bear anymore, but the more I think about it, I just can't imagine that he would willingly go anywhere without making sure that bear was with him." Charlotte grew more confident in her interpretation of the events with every breath.

"Err, Charlotte, I am not sure I am following you."

"The police asked me before if I saw anything suspicious in the house, and at the time I said no, that I hadn't. But now I do!"

"What exactly are you saying?"

"I'm saying that someone or something forced them to go, and Fletcher must have put the fire truck in the freezer as a way of telling me what happened without jeopardizing Jake! He didn't kidnap Jake! They both were kidnapped!"

Chapter 12

To one who has faith, no explanation is necessary. To one without faith, no explanation is possible.

—Thomas Aquinas

Successfully rendering her mother speechless, Charlotte drove back down to the police station to present them with her new evidence. Once again, she was asked to wait along the row of bolted-down chairs until an officer could meet with her. She of course would have been more relieved if she had actually found her husband and son, but she believed that now that she had a better case for an involuntary absence, the police might be more willing to spend additional resources on locating them.

Charlotte felt that she even had a suspect. She would tell them all about the threatening e-mail between Fletcher and Marshall. Her time at Fletcher's office would not have been in vain. The police would track Marshall down, and they would find Fletcher and Jake—shaken and bruised, yes, but safe and sound in some cousin's house.

The same officer she had spoken with before met her in the doorway and brought her back among the desks. "You know, you really didn't have to come all the way down here, Mrs. Row. Nothing has changed since we last spoke on the phone, and I warned you that we only had limited resources."

"Fletcher didn't take Jake. Someone took them both, and I have a name for you to follow up on." Charlotte beamed; she could feel in her heart that her family would be home with her again before the end of the day.

The officer pulled out his notepad. "And what evidence did you find that has led you to this conclusion?"

Charlotte told the officer about Mr. Snaps, the fire truck in the freezer, and her and Fletcher's plan for an emergency secret code. As she spoke, a part of her noticed that the officer's pen had lain mostly dormant alongside the pad. She began to become slightly apprehensive. When she had been home and explained her interpretation of events to her mother, it was as if Fletcher had left her neon-bright signs. Now, she realized that she might be coming off as potentially unhinged.

"So nothing else was damaged or out of place except for some toys?"

"Um, not that I noticed. There might have been more, but my mom cleaned my house up and nothing is where it used to be. I know this all sounds crazy, but I am sure he was sending me a message!"

"You mentioned that you thought you had a suspect's name too?"

"Oh yes. I had gone to Fletchers office to see what appointments he might have had and to see why he might have needed a separate savings account, and I came across a string of threatening e-mail messages from a subcontractor named Marshall Thomas."

"And why was this Marshall Thomas threatening him?"

"Well, according to the messages, he claimed that Fletcher owed him some money."

"And did he?"

"Fletcher claimed he didn't. He said that Marshall didn't complete the work and so wasn't owed anything. Marshall said that Fletcher shouldn't mess with him, and that he was going to come down to the office to collect."

"And did he?"

"He did, only my husband wasn't there at the time. He had been out making sales calls."

"Who was there?"

"His receptionist and a woman from inside sales."

"And did you ask either of these people what happened while he was at the office? What this Marshall's demeanor might have been?"

Charlotte realized that she actually had not followed up with Stacey at all about the event. After the coffee and pen incident, she really had just wanted to avoid Stacey altogether to focus on her investigation, and then Stacey had had that family emergency that she needed to run off to.

"I didn't ask. All I know is that Fletcher had to call you guys in to escort him off the premises."

"Well, that's something. Do you happen to know when this event might have taken place?"

"Only that it was maybe two, three weeks ago?"

"I see."

Charlotte began to feel like perhaps she didn't have quite as solid a case as she thought she had when she first entered the station. Even the part about Marshall's threats seemed somewhat flimsy.

The officer scribbled a few notes onto his pad, put his pen down, and looked at Charlotte. "Well, I can't say that this is a lot to go on, but I will at least look into the incident at his office and see if there is anything in the report that would suggest this Marshall person is out for a more serious revenge. In the meantime, you mentioned that your mother is around. It might be a good idea not to spend too much time alone. Being alone in such as stressful situation would make anyone see things that aren't necessarily there."

"You don't believe me." Charlotte bowed her head dejectedly.

"I'm not saying that. We will look into the incident at the office as I said. I just want to caution you not to get your hopes up. I don't want to unnecessarily worry you though, but if this Marshall is the type to take revenge, then you also have to ready yourself to the possibility that he didn't just settle for kidnapping your family, especially after nearly a week."

The police officer must have recognized the state of panic and shock on Charlotte's features. Charlotte's imaginings had not let her even consider terminal possibilities. "Mrs. Row, I am sorry if you weren't ready to hear that, but you do need to understand how this could play out if your theory is correct. Can I call someone to come and pick you up? Your mother, maybe?"

"No, not my mother," Charlotte's voice was a bare whisper. Her mother had been too ready to believe the worst about her husband. Charlotte didn't fault her mom, at least not entirely. She did understand that her mother just wanted to protect and champion her, but she needed to go where someone would be as equally concerned about Fletcher's disappearance as Jake's. "Marie. Can you call my friend Marie?"

A short time later, Marie came blazing into the police station waving one of the flyers that Charlotte's mother and sister must have posted.

"Oh my god, Charlotte! After we didn't hear back from you about trying to track Fletcher down, we just assumed he made it home. Why didn't you call me back and told me what was going on?" Charlotte was ashamed that she had never had the guts to reach out to any of her friends. She had been too mortified to admit to them that things in her life weren't picture perfect, that out of the four of them, she was the one whose relationship was in jeopardy.

Marie continued, either not noticing Charlotte's shame or at least forgiving enough not to call attention to it. "I've seen these all over town, and now I am getting calls asking to pick you up from the police. What is going on?"

When Charlotte saw her friend's look of concern, she felt as if the floor had dropped out from under her feet and wrapped her arms around her friend as she starting crying once again. She had been feeling so confident thinking that she was on her way to finding her family and having her life return to normal when she woke up this morning, but that scab had been picked and was now gushing anew. Charlotte couldn't speak; the only sounds that emerged from her throat were gasps.

"Shh, shh, Charlotte. We'll take you out of here. Tom is with me and will drive your car to our place. Can you point to where you parked?" Charlotte waved her hand in the general direction of where her car was parked, and Marie rifled through Charlotte's purse in search of her keys with one hand while supporting Charlotte with the other. As Marie had mentioned, Tom was there, tall and muscled, but reduced to a paralyzed weakling when faced with a woman crying in complete abandon.

Eventually, they pulled into Tom and Marie's driveway, Marie leading Charlotte inside and sitting her down at the couch, but not leaving her side.

"Tom, how about you pour some tea or something for Charlotte and bring out some crackers."

Tom jumped to action and nearly ran into the kitchen, eager to escape the room yet still help in some way. Their couch was a relic, one of the first pieces of furniture any of the group had bought in their post-college days, and had been generally abused throughout the year's game nights and sporting event viewings. A particular stain on the ridge of one of the couch cushions caught Charlotte's eye, and she stared at it intently, not really noticing that her surroundings had changed.

"Charlotte, Charlotte, come back." Marie rubbed Charlotte's hand, and when that didn't work, snapped her fingers. "Charlotte, what is going on? We started seeing these flyers everywhere, and I mean *everywhere*. What happened?"

Tom nervously set a glass of iced tea on the coffee table in front of Charlotte, as if afraid that the slightest motion might restart the waterworks. The glass was no sooner down than he was returning to the kitchen in search of the crackers. The sound of glass on glass brought Charlotte back to the present.

"Oh, Marie, after we got back from our trip, they were gone. Not just Jake, Fletcher too. The police think Fletcher took Jake and left me, but I know something has happened to them. Fletcher had a secret bank account, and he hasn't told me half of what was going on at his work. I also found threatening messages from a guy who was seriously pissed off at him. Mr. Snaps was at the house! You know Jake wouldn't leave without Mr. Snaps! I told you about that road trip from hell! Something's happened to them! They're missing and could be dead!"

"Charlotte, explain it again slowly for me this time." Charlotte had never seen her friend quite so serious in her expression. It looked as foreign on her face as Tom's careful nervousness had.

Charlotte attempted to calm her breathing and started from the beginning, telling her friend all the details, including all about her mom's attempt at bettering her life through home organization and the strangely placed fire truck.

"I know he was telling me something." Charlotte looked for any sign—an eye roll, a knowing tilt to her head in Tom's direction, anything that might indicate that Charlotte made a mistake in calling her friends for support. However, if Marie thought that Charlotte was jumping to impossible conclusions, she kept that thought securely bolted down inside.

"Well, if he was, then he might still be okay."

"What do you mean?"

"Think about it, Charlotte, if he had time to go to your kitchen, then whoever took him wasn't exactly rushing into your house and taking them unawares. He was making conscious decisions, which means he probably left on his own two feet, and you know there would have been signs of violence if Jake had been hurt."

Charlotte looked at her friend in amazement. She hadn't made that connection, but there was some solid logic to Marie's argument. Tom had returned from the kitchen with a plate of crackers, which he placed in front of the ladies, and sat down on one of the chairs across from them.

"Did you see any sign of a ransom note or anything?"

"No, nothing like that. I mean, there could have been, but my mom moved everything."

"Yeah, but you would have thought she would have noticed something like that, right?" suggested Marie.

"I would have thought so, but she has been so sold on thinking that Fletcher is a bum and left me that I don't know if she would have noticed anything like that or not."

"But you don't think so. You think this Marshall person is involved?" asked Tom, better able to cope with a more rational version of Charlotte.

"Maybe? I don't know. Supposedly he had gone to Fletcher's office to collect his money, and the police were called. Fletcher wasn't there. Maybe he decided to follow him home one night."

"Charlotte, you do know that Fletcher has received that kind of messages before, right? There always seems to be someone asking for money or an advance or something. When we play basketball, he tells me all sorts of stories about the crazy people he has come into contact with ever since he started going into business for himself. From what you've told me, Marshall doesn't even sound like he is in the top ten."

"No, he hadn't told me any of that." At least Charlotte didn't think Fletcher had told her, the past few days had proven though that she had been at least half as guilty as Fletcher was at tuning the other out.

"Oh yeah, he has told me some great stories. For example, did he ever tell you about Regan and her daughter?"

"Ummm, no?"

"So this Regan lady has been married like four or five times and has this daughter from either the second or third marriage, I don't quite remember. Anyway, the way Fletch told me was that he got a call from Regan one day, saying that she wasn't going to be able to come to work that day. Apparently, her daughter was visiting and was accusing her of neglecting her during her childhood while Regan was married to one of her stepdads. Later on, he gets this call—it's Regan, only this time she is telling Fletcher that her daughter has come at her with a knife, that she has locked herself in her bedroom, and would Fletcher please come and help because she doesn't want to further alienate her daughter by calling the police."

"He never told me anything like that! Did he go?" Charlotte was shocked and appalled that not only had her husband put himself in a potentially emotionally charged and violent situation, it was apparently such a non-event for him that he hadn't even mentioned it to her.

"Yeah, he did. I told him he was nuts when he told me. I told him I would have called the police, but he just shrugged and said that when he got there, everything was fine. There was some clothing and furniture outside on the lawn, which he helped bring back in. Regan was still locked in her bedroom, but the daughter seemed to be okay, and there was no sign of a knife anywhere. Fletcher told me that the following day, Regan was back in the office, happy as can be, like nothing out of the normal had happened at all. Then she told Fletcher that she was going to take the next week off so that she and her daughter could take a cruise together."

"What was he thinking? The daughter could have just as easily gone after him! Wait? When did this all happen? Do you think the daughter could have come back for him?" demanded Charlotte.

"I doubt it. This all happened last year, and he said that after the cruise, Regan mentioned that her daughter was returning to Florida. She's somehow tied to the medical profession. Isn't that scary? At least she has access to meds. Fletcher hadn't brought her up with me since then, so I would assume she hasn't been back, but I wouldn't know that for sure."

After she had calmed, not wanting to keep her friends from their own jobs any longer, Charlotte thanked them for their help and returned to Fletcher's office in order to ask Stacey more about the day Marshall came in with his demands and to ask Daniel if there was ever another incident with Regan's daughter. Stacey was on the phone when she arrived but smiled, handed her a stack of envelopes, and waved her through the door, silently mouthing, "Sorry about yesterday."

Charlotte took the stack of envelopes back to Fletcher's desk and decided to open them while she waited for the red light on the phone to turn off, which would signal that Stacey was free. Charlotte was very surprised to see, upon opening them, that nearly all contained checks. She fired up Fletcher's computer and also saw e-mail confirmations of direct deposits totaling several thousands of dollars.

The red light blinked off, and Charlotte seized the chance to return to the front desk to speak with Stacey. Not wishing to come across as uncaring, which might make Stacey not willing to be as open with her as possible, Charlotte asked about Stacey's emergency from the day before.

"How is your son? Is he going to be able to stay in school?"

"Only a suspension this time. He is staying today with his aunt. I don't know what is wrong with that kid. Ever since his father was called back to active service, he's been acting out. This isn't the first time his father's been away. I just don't know what to do with him anymore! I was hoping that he might be interested in helping out here with the Cell Phone for Soldiers campaign. You are still collecting phones starting tomorrow?" Charlotte nodded. "I thought maybe he could draw some posters, sort through some phones, or something like that, but when I asked him about, it he stormed off. I am having to remove all the doors in my house, he keeps slamming them. One of these past days, his little sister was going to get too close, and he was going to hurt her. And now he is fighting with kids at school and getting into all sorts of other trouble."

"Umm, Stacey, I somewhat hate to bring this up, but speaking of trouble, I understand that you were here a few weeks back when a subcontractor named Marshall came in demanding money. Is that true?"

"Oh yeah, irritating man. He just sat there glaring at everyone who came in. I told him that Fletcher was out of the office, and he said he was going to wait around until he came back. I called Fletcher about it, and he asked me to call the police to have him escorted out. I didn't know why he was there though. He spoke with Regan some, but he only talked when he was demanding to see Fletcher."

"So he didn't threaten you?"

"Hardly. My son could do more damage to that man than he could do to me, skinny nerdy type, you know? Besides, my husband made sure that I knew how to defend myself before he left."

"Did Regan tell you what they talked about?"

"Only that he was down on his luck. I really didn't ask. I was always the one stuck doing the majority of Regan's work whenever she called in with a *sick* day." Stacey didn't need to actually perform the air quotes around the word "sick"— Charlotte could practically taste the sarcasm. It was clear to Charlotte that Regan and Stacey were not the closest of friends, and that Stacey most likely would not have been the one that Regan would have confided to if there were any additional concerns about her daughter.

Daniel walked up behind Charlotte at that moment, practically dancing on his way to the door. "Oh hey, Charlotte. Any news?" he asked.

"No. No news really since yesterday, I'm following up on a few more leads today."

"Me too!" His eyes were alight. "I've got great news. You remember that call I took yesterday? Avnex Corporation? Well, after I spoke with them yesterday morning, I went over to make an initial meeting yesterday afternoon. And now they want me back for a large-scale presentation. We are talking about a multi-year potential contract across a number of their subsidiary companies! We've been chasing after this account for months, and the decision makers are all going to be there. This could be a game changer!"

"That would be great," said Charlotte, and she truly did mean it. She was glad to hear some positive news for a change, but she was saddened that Fletcher wasn't there to see that his dream might potentially come to fruition—even if it was only yet a glimmer on the horizon.

Daniel's tone briefly softened, "You just have to keep the faith, Charlotte." The moment passed, and he continued to walk triumphantly out the door. Stacey shouted, "You land this account and lunch will be on me!" To which he replied, "Oh, I will. I'm so sure about this one. I'll even watch your kids for a night if they don't sign!"

Charlotte followed him out of the office and into the parking lot. "Daniel, just a quick question before you go. Did Regan ever tell you about any issues with her daughter?"

Daniel looked at Charlotte slightly confused, "Regan's daughter? No, I haven't heard anything about her lately. Regan mentioned going on a cruise with her awhile back, but no, nothing else.

"Oh, okay, well, thanks anyway. So this presentation really could make a difference?"

"Oh yeah, a copy of the proposal is on my computer. You should check it out."

"Thanks for your help. Oh, and thanks for not asking about Fletcher or Jake in front of Stacey. I haven't quite figured out how much to tell her."

"Yeah, I wasn't too sure how much you wanted to share. We're at the verge of greatness here. You don't want to risk messing it up!"

"Well, again, good luck."

"Good luck to you too."

Chapter 13

It is not in the stars to hold our destiny but in ourselves.
—William Shakespeare

Stacey's comments regarding the physical prowess of Marshall weighed down upon Charlotte as she reentered the office. The police had said that they would investigate him, and so she might not have any choice but to wait for another update from them. Starved for good news after being faced with so many dead leads, Charlotte printed out a copy of Daniel's proposal for Avnex Corporation and returned to Fletcher's desk.

She scanned through the multi-page proposal. The name Avnex started to gnaw on her, and at first she didn't fully understand why. Then she started to look through the proposal before her. Avnex wasn't exactly a household brand name, and she was startled by the number of people connected to the organization and the breadth of their reach. Their organization had derivatives in dozens of enterprises—not just within the area, but across many states. A win such as this would give Fletcher's platform regional-wide exposure, except something felt wrong about the document. It just did not feel complete.

She cleared her head much as she did whenever she attempted to complete a research project. She took a cleansing breath, then another. She closed her eyes, and suddenly all the connections were crystal clear, as well as the connections that weren't in the proposal—the glaring holes. Fletcher's proposal, structured as it was, could result in a few years of regional gains; but if she was correct and could amend the document before Daniel presented it, Archer Service Solutions could go national.

Had the case been a patent inquiry that could be charged back to a client, she would have been rock solid in her conviction, but this was not her standard industry, and she hated to risk potentially jeopardizing the deal without at least a sanity check. She had to make certain that she was running the numbers in her head correctly to account for overhead and resources needed to support such a proposal. As Fletcher obviously wasn't going to magically make himself available to perform this service, she called Mr. Peace and e-mailed him and Daniel a copy of the original and the amended document.

"Hello, Charlotte. Yes, I've heard of Avnex Corporation. Fletcher had mentioned that he has been chasing that account for quite some time. I have to agree with your assessment. If you add in the changes you are suggesting, then it will be a rock-solid proposal. When is the meeting?"

"Daniel was on his way. It may be going on right now."

"Do you think you can make the changes in time?"

"I've got Stacey on standby. Now that I've heard from you, I am giving her the signal to send a quick message to Daniel and have him deliver the updated proposal." Charlotte waved to a ready and waiting Stacey who quickly hurried off to her desk to complete the task.

"And he believes he is meeting with the decision makers?"

"I believe so."

"Well, do you have any idea what their decision-making process might be? Do you think they will need to have several rounds of proposals, or do you think they might be ready to make a quick decision?"

"Er . . . he really didn't say, but they put together this second meeting fairly quickly. I would assume that they are fairly interested."

"Oh, they called him?"

"Yesterday. The initial meeting was yesterday, and the larger presentation today."

"Yes, it does sound like they are motivated. Well, that's good news."

"It is, isn't it? I mean, we can handle winning something like this, right?"

"Well, assuming that you do in fact win the business. And, Charlotte, as motivated as they might seem right now, there is no guarantee that you will win the business. They might be taking other meetings with the same sense of urgency. But if we were to speculate that you were indeed awarded the business, the added exposure of such a contract would reduce the marketing investment you might need to make, but only slightly as a lot of companies aren't exactly happy to let their competitors know who their suppliers are. You would still need to upgrade your equipment though. In fact, that would become a high priority concern. A few years ago, this proposal, signed, probably would have gotten you a bank loan for the upgrades, but now you may have to get a little creative. Before you ask though, I need to also caution you that no one is going to enter into a contract like this without doing a lot of due diligence on the strength of the company it is considering partnering with. They are not going to be interested doing business with a company whose leadership is not firmly involved in the day to day and is available at their beck and call. Charlotte, I've seen the flyers around town about Jake. And since you are calling me instead of Fletcher about a fairly standard, albeit large, service contract, I must assume he is also missing. Have you heard anything at all about where they might have gone?"

"I've been in contact with the police, and they have a few leads, but no, nothing solid yet."

"I see. I'm really sorry to hear that. I know you must be worried sick."

"I am. I really, really am. I'm just trying to keep myself somewhat distracted. If I think on it too much, I'm lost."

"Well, is running Archer Service Solutions something that you think you might be able to focus on for now?"

"I really don't know. It was always Fletcher's dream, not mine. And truthfully, I am finding out that I might not know the first thing about what he was dealing with day in and day out."

"The reason I ask is, if you aren't, then this proposal isn't worth anything. But if you are, well then, based on this, there is a chance that Fletcher's dream might still live on. It is going to be up to you."

***

Charlotte had no sooner hung up the phone with Frank Peace than the line rung again.

"Charlotte, I have a Peter Demsey on the phone for you. He says he and you have spoken before?"

Unsure why he might be calling her, Charlotte agreed to accept the call. "Ah, good. I wasn't sure if you were going to be back in the office today or not."

"Hi, Peter. Yes, I came in to follow up on a few leads."

"I saw the flyers. You can sure tell who his parents are. The brown hair from you, I assume? Otherwise, he looks just like his dad. No updates?"

Peter continued as his momentary pause went without answer.

"Well . . . let me just jump right to the reason I called. I mentioned that I had a client that might be interested in selling their company, and I am happy to report that there is interest out there. Not a lot, but there is at least one contact that is willing to throw out a number. The only thing is that this contact has already done its homework. They know about your personal distraction and the fact that the company is lacking strong leadership. I don't want you to think that by accepting this offer, all your problems are going to be solved—it's really an offer just for the platform itself. If you were to accept it, Archer Service Solutions would cease to be, but you would at least get your initial investment back. I believe Fletcher once told me that you had invested most, if not all, of your personal retirement savings into getting this started up?"

"So if we were to take this offer, you are telling me we would be back to where we started from five years ago."

"That's correct."

"But with nothing else to show for the sacrifices we've made?"

"Well, no."

"And I'd still need to work at my current job?"

"I am not saying you have to stay at your current job if you are unhappy there, but yes, you would need to find another source of recurring income if you left. Eh, I know you are not going to like hearing this, but with your current situation, your expenses should be less. You might be able to make the payout go much further than you might have previously."

"My situation?"

"Well, you are only going to have to support yourself now, aren't you?"

"Ahh . . . I see . . . you've given me a lot to think on."

"Think on it over the weekend, and give me a callback. If you'd like to hear more, I will notify my contact to write up a more formal offer."

Charlotte hung up the phone, disgusted by Peter's suggestion that she might somehow be better off without her family. Most of her wanted to refuse the offer immediately out of principle alone, but as odious as she found him, it might be better than losing everything.

Charlotte wondered aloud to herself if Richard might actually seem sensitive in comparison to Peter. As if summoned like a demon in a black magic ceremony, the phone rang once again, with Stacey identifying Richard on the other end of the line. Unsure as to whether or not she truly wanted to take the call, she hesitated before agreeing that she would accept the transfer. Charlotte actually wasn't exactly sure how Richard had obtained this number. He must have looked at and tried her emergency contact numbers from her personnel file—a degree of effort on his part that one might interpret as a sign of how much he missed her around the office, but more likely indicated the depth of his displeasure in her continued absence.

"Charlotte, it's Richard. I thought that during our last conversation I made it clear that I expected progress reports."

"You did, and I am sorry I haven't checked in yet."

"So everything has been taken care of and you'll be back in tomorrow?"

"Err . . . no, no. My family is still missing."

"Oh? So not tomorrow, Monday then?"

"Eh, maybe? I don't really know. I can try, but I might not be totally focused. Do you think I might be able to phase back in next week part-time?"

"Charlotte, this is not a part-time position, and it's not fair to the other staff for me to give you special treatment."

"I'm not asking for special treatment. I just might need a little more time to follow up on a few more leads."

"Are the police not involved?"

"They are, but—"

"And you would agree that they are paid professionals with resources—that you lack—at their disposal, yes?"

"Well, yes, but—"

"But you think you can do a better job than they can with your lack of experience."

"It's not that! I just—"

"Charlotte, I know you are a researcher, and I will say that you do an adequate job. But there is a reason that companies use people like us to determine whether or not they have a patentable product. It's because we have experience they lack. They trust us to do a thorough review of their case and make solid recommendations. It is what they pay us to do."

"I know, but you don't understand!"

"I understand that we require research done so that we can make our recommendations, a job that I currently pay you to do. But you are telling me that you are too busy doing a job that we as taxpayers pay others more experienced than you to do. To me, that sounds like you might be exercising poor judgment. And I am not sure that we can continue to keep someone like that on the payroll when there are other more capable individuals in need of just such a position."

"Are you saying that you are letting me go?"

"I am saying that you, Charlotte, have a serious choice to make. This weekend is an opportunity for you to really think long and hard about where you want to be. I do, however, want you to recognize that I do not have infinite patience, and that I fully expect to see you at your desk on Monday or a call regarding where to send your things."

Chapter 14

Deep into that darkness peering, long I stood there, wondering, fearing, doubting, dreaming dreams no mortal ever dared to dream before.

—Edgar Allan Poe

Later that evening when she returned home, she was met at the door by Beth holding a bag of carryout from their mutually favorite restaurant. One of the unanticipated benefits of requesting that Marie pick her up from the police station was that she was saved from bringing all of their other friends up to speed. Marie was a communication hub incarnate and would have shared with Beth not only the facts regarding Charlotte's family, but would have also informed everyone about the color of paint on the walls in the station, along with how many lights Tom ran on their way to pick her up.

The two entered the house and sat down at the kitchen still without exchanging words. Charlotte's stomach grumbled as Beth opened the bag, allowing the smell of greasy comfort food to permeate throughout the room. The food, though delicious-smelling in the air, tasted like Styrofoam in her mouth. As quickly as her appetite had made its appearance, it was gone just as completely again. She stared at the full plate in front of her, but made no further effort to clear it.

Beth looked at Charlotte's plate. "Now, Charlotte, you know you need to keep your strength up. You are going to have to eat."

"Sorry, I know, but I am really just not hungry."

"Can you try to eat something, if not for yourself, for me?"

"I appreciate you bringing it over. I really do. It just doesn't taste right tonight."

"How about five bites?" Beth asked this with only the slightest smile on her lips. Charlotte found herself mirroring Beth's expression, recognizing the subtle reference to her frequent complaints about her and Jake's dinner time routine.

"Are you ready to talk about it?" asked Beth, no longer teasing.

"Do you think my mom is right? Am I just living in denial?"

"She's that certain?"

"She's nearly had the papers written up for me, and I still don't know for certain what happened. If Fletcher took off with Jake, they have such a head start that I might not ever see him again. But at least Jake is most likely okay and probably happy to have so much of his dad's undivided attention. He probably wouldn't even be missing me yet. Eventually he would though, and when that happens, Fletcher would have to relent and let me at least talk to him."

"But . . . you don't think he took him."

"No." And Charlotte bowed her head in defeat. "No, I don't. I've tried and tried to make sense of it, but it just doesn't match up. Meaning, I might now have lost them both, and yet all I hear from my mom is how much I should hate him. I just don't know what to believe. I don't know what to do! I've never been this unsure of anything in my life! I thought that if I just lead the investigation, then at least I would be doing something productive. But all I've done is chase a bunch of dead ends. Fletcher is gone, Jake is gone, Fletcher's business could potentially be going up in smoke, and now my job might even be on the line."

"How is your job on the line?"

"Richard. He made it very clear that if I'm not back in the very near future, then I might as well not come back at all."

"Does he not know what is going on?"

"He does, but he called it a personal problem."

"A personal problem?" Beth's eyebrows shot up nearly to the top of her scalp. "I would say that this is a slightly bigger deal than a sick day. I thought you had all that time saved up?"

"I've saved up a couple of weeks, but not a huge bank of time—day care sick days really ate into that. Fletcher was never able to stay home with him more than a couple of hours. If he wasn't out selling, no one was, but that really doesn't matter. Hardly anyone at my office ever gets to take a vacation, certainly never anything last minute."

"You're not asking to take a vacation though. I can't believe he's not being more understanding. What a jerk!"

All Charlotte could do is shrug. Her limited exposure to Fletcher's business had shown her how draining unproductive employees could be, but at the same time, she just couldn't find it in her heart to be overtly sympathetic. She thought on her limited options. She could get rid of Fletcher's business and go back to her job—or something else exactly like it—allowing her life to pass her by as she waited by the phone for a call from the police that may or may never happen, sneaking in time for her own investigation or going further into debt by outsourcing it. Of course, she could take on the risk of Fletcher's business in the hope it might stay alive until he comes back—if he comes back. Archer Service Solutions was always his dream, not hers.

She must have spoken at least a portion of her internal musings out loud as Beth spoke up, "You could always make it your dream too, you know."

That night after Beth left, Charlotte tossed and turned, eventually succumbing to sleep. In her dream, she was imprisoned high in the tower, a beast that vaguely resembled Richard guarding the keep below. She was able to look through a single small window, but though she ran around the turret, she was unable to find a door or any other means of escaping. Through that small window, she saw Fletcher appear far below, challenging the beast. He charged at the monster—it reared its awful head along with its massive claws. Charlotte saw the claws descend as if in slow motion. As they did so, she looked toward herself, unable to watch the battle.

She blinked and was wearing her bridal gown. It was the day of her and Fletcher's wedding. She had watched him as she made her way down the aisle tilt his head in her direction as he smiled from ear to ear. In her dream the church had taken on the proportions of Westminster Abbey, and she had felt as proud as a princess, each step bringing them closer together. Music blared from the organ pipes, and all around her were tears of joy from their friends and family.

In the way of dreams, Jake was there, bridging the distance between her and Fletcher; and suddenly there was no distance between them at all. He continued playing with fire trucks and Mr. Snaps as the ceremony continued.

As Charlotte approached the altar, Jake stood up and began to address the entire congregation. "Dearly beloved, here we are. Daddy, do you love Mommy? Will you share your toys and your joys on good days and on grumpy days?"

Fletcher gazed at Charlotte, the gentle rainbow light from the stain-glassed window resting on his head, his features taking on the same boyish joy as she now saw on Jake's face most days. "I will."

"And Mommy, do you love Daddy? Will you share your toys and your joys on good days and on grumpy days?"

Charlotte gazed back at Fletcher. Suddenly, they were in the hospital, and it was the day Jake was born. The labor had been long and difficult, and she had been exhausted when it was finally complete. Too exhausted to trust herself with the newborn infant, and more than a little panicked when the nurses placed him on her breast. Without needing to ask, Fletcher had picked up the noisy bundle and rocked him patiently until she was brave enough to take him back. As he laid the baby back down, he helped brush her hair back.

Then it was the evening of New Year's Eve, and she was at a jam-packed party over at Marie's apartment which surly violated fire codes. The crowd shouted, "10, 9, 8!" Marie had handed out confetti shooters shaped like Champagne bottles, "7, 6, 5," Tom handed out noise makers and party hats, "4, 3, 2, 1!" One of the confetti shooters accidentally launched along with its paper contents, hitting Charlotte by the side of her head. The overly exuberant reliever had embarrassedly come her way to see the damage from his clumsiness. Her eyes met Fletcher's as he brushed her hair back while he apologized profusely and inspected the damage. She hadn't heard a word he had spoken. They had gone outside, huddled shoulder to shoulder in order to consolidate warmth during the winter evening and to hear each other better; but those words too were lost, drowned out by the fireworks launching in the night sky.

They remained side by side, but now it could be any regular evening at home. Dinner already completed, Jake played contentedly in the den as she scrubbed the dishes while Fletcher dried and put them away. Feeling playful, she splashed some of the soapy water in his general direction. He retaliated by scooping up some leftover mashed potatoes, taking aim at her like he was loading a catapult. She squealed in delight as she ran, placing a very confused Jake between the potatopult and herself. Jake, picking a side, spun around and held his mother in place while Fletcher flung the potatoes at them both. It rapidly became a full-scale food fight, ending only with all three of them laughing exhaustedly as they collapsed together in a heap of bubbles and leftovers.

She turned toward Fletcher and whispered, "I will."

"Kiss for you Mommy!" Charlotte was back at home tucking Jake into his bed. She leaned in to give him another kiss on his forehead, only he was no longer paying her any attention. Instead he was playing on his dad's cell phone. "Look, Mom! Look what I drew!" She looked—there on the screen was a fire truck.

Charlotte smiled at the drawing with pride. She rose from the bed. It was now a hospital bed occupied by Fletcher. A nurse brought in a stack of papers, dropping them on his chest. Without being asked, Charlotte collected the papers, taking them over to a nearby rocking chair to sort through while Fletcher recovered from his ordeal. Fletcher reached toward her with an outstretched hand. They were at the beach. A huge wave stirred in the distance, rapidly charging toward them. Their hands clasped together as the wave began its descent, and she awoke.

Chapter 15

How much pain they have cost us, the evils which have never happened.

—Thomas Jefferson

Charlotte stretched in the morning dawn, her head no longer aching from excess alcohol or bottomless tears. She realized that at some point during the night, she had reached a decision, at least on the only part of her life as she knew it that she still had some degree of control over. She entered Jake's room hoping to find Fletcher's old cell phone—the one he had said was going to be donated, although they both knew full well that Jake would have fought tooth and nail to keep his newest "toy."

The dream last night had reminded her that there was a plethora of Jake's artwork still stored on the device, most of which had no resemblance to the fire truck in her dream, but were each masterpieces—especially now. She would donate the phone, as it was a worthy cause, but first she would make sure to download each and every one of them. Unfortunately, the device would not power up, so she was forced to hunt through the house for any spare power adapter and leave the phone on its charger while she finished getting ready to face the rest of the day.

After what seemed like an eternity, the indicator light on the phone finally changed from red to green, and the screen lit up with a painfully slow start-up sequence. Jake's smiling face appeared on the wallpaper. An alert flashed informing her that the phone was no longer supported by a cellular network. She just hoped that Jake's artwork had been stored on the phone's memory alone and not on any external SIM card.

She attempted to navigate her way through the phone's folder structure, increasingly getting annoyed that the files she so desperately wanted to see were so elusive. Charlotte gave up on trying to bring the images up using the phone's interface. She was going to download the images onto a computer anyway, so hooking it up to her computer and finding them using the medium that she was most confident with made the most sense. Unfortunately, none of the cables were readily available at her house; she was going to have to wait until she drove into Fletcher's office.

Nearly an hour later, she was back behind Fletcher's desk—computer whirling as it completed its connection to the device. A message appearing in the lower right hand corner of the window told her that there were still pieces of Jake mixed within the assortment of copper and silicone. She eagerly clicked through the resulting folder structure and nearly cried when she saw that the files she was looking for were still indeed there.

Her screen was filled up with nonsensical swirls of blue and green and yellow, each more wondrous than the last. Each triggered memories, within Charlotte, of times when she and Fletcher had been both too busy with what they thought were more important things when they had given him the phone to draw on as last-ditch attempt to distract him. Her eyes began to tear up once again, only this time she would not allow them to blind her. She scrolled through each a dozen more times before saving them to the computer's hard drive for later retrieval. Once on the hard drive, she accessed them all a few dozen times more just to ensure that they had been safely moved.

Satisfied that she was not going to cause permanent damage, she began to search online how to successfully wipe a phone's memory bank prior to sale or donation. A comment in the article caught her eye. In it, the article cautioned that even a phone's text messages could still be accessed even after the phone's service contract ended depending on how the data had been stored on the device. The comment gave Charlotte reason to pause. If Jake's drawings were still on the phone, could some of her and Fletcher's old text messages still be there as well? She might still have a digital piece of him to save alongside of her son.

Charlotte returned to the phone and its cursed unfriendly user interface and accessed the text message menu screen. Segments of the last message in various conversational strings appeared on the screen. One of the last messages listed was not between Fletcher and herself, but between him and Regan.

"Fletcher, I'm not coming in today."

"Why not?"

"You know why not."

"Please enlighten me."

"It's another one of those days. I'm going into a dark place right now."

"Regan, I have a business to run.
These absences are unfair to everyone else.
I need to know I can count on you.
If I can't count on you . . ."

"I'm your best performer. You know that I am."

"I am not arguing that you don't hit
your numbers when you are here."

"You wouldn't have made it this long without me."

"Regan, this is not a personal decision."

"No one likes me there.

That bitch has turned you against me."

"What?"

"You know who!"

"No, frankly I don't. Please keep this professional.
Why don't you come in and we can have this
conversation face-to-face?"

"So that F B can turn her nose up. I don't think so."

"Fine. If you can't be respectful,
that's it. We're done."

"You are such a fraud. I am going to expose you!"

"I don't know what you are talking about.
It doesn't matter though.
My decision has been made, and it is final."

"You'll be sorry!

"I will not be a victim!"

"Please stop writing me."

"It's on!"

Charlotte glanced at the message's time and date stamp. The entire conversation spanned several hours in length, Regan sending message after message. In some messages, she sounded like a pitiful victim of circumstances and hearsay who was being cut adrift without a life raft of any kind. In others, she described Fletcher as a fat, sexist pig, intentionally singling her out because she wouldn't agree to be his personal secretary. When Fletcher did not respond to this line of accusation, she switched tactics, lamenting how difficult it was going to be for a woman of her age to find employment elsewhere. This also went unanswered by Fletcher.

She then threw out accusations of age discrimination and racism. It was almost as if she was going through a textbook of any potential accusation a person could make to fight a wrongful termination suit even though Fletcher was operating his business in a right to work state. She repeated that Fletcher would be nowhere without her and that she was going to laugh when his business went up in flames. Eventually run out of creative ideas for accusations, her messages continued well into the early hours of the morning—unanswered and containing nothing but a few random characters as if her intent was to slowly annoy Fletcher, who typically kept his phone on for emergency purposes, by the incessant sound of the alert notification.

As Charlotte did not remember a particularly long evening of beeps and buzzes emanating off of Fletcher's phone, he must have risked potentially not responding to an emergency in a timely manner by silencing the alert. She also noted that

Fletcher must have gone out and purchased his replacement phone the following day. Charlotte wondered how much the text message exchange with Regan played into his decision-making process as to what phone to buy and features to consider.

Charlotte placed the phone down next to the desk. She had been curious to learn more about the altercation with Marshall from Regan's perspective, but now she was not exactly sure that Regan would be the most reliable of witnesses, especially as hostile and petty as she seemed from this particular message string. She was also nervous about potentially embarking on yet another wild goose chase; she decided to ask for a second opinion.

"Daniel, do you have a second?"

"Sure, what is it?"

"Well, I'm not really sure it's anything at all. I was clearing up Fletcher's old cell phone so that we could donate it and came across an odd conversation between Fletcher and Regan. Can you tell me when her last day was?"

"She just stopped coming in one day. It was a day or so after the Marshall incident. Was that really less than two weeks ago? It seems longer."

"And did Fletcher ever mention why?"

"No, he didn't. But as you know, that was pretty regular behavior for Regan."

"Do you know if Fletcher ever tried to talk to her about it or discipline her in anyway?"

"He might have. I really don't know. If he did, he didn't share it with me. But he might have put something in her personnel file, right? I mean, that is what you are supposed to do, isn't it?"

"Ah, yes, I'll check there. Are you heading back out into the field today?"

"Friday is typically my office day. I like to research my accounts, make a few calls, e-mail a few proposals, and plan for the next week—that sort of thing."

"Okay, so if I need you, will you be around?"

"Just a shout away."

Chapter 16

*A strong woman is a woman determined to do
something others are determined not be done.*

—Marge Piercy

After Daniel departed, Charlotte searched around Fletcher's
desk for whatever personnel files he might possess. One of the
filing cabinets was locked, and she assumed that what she was
looking for had to be located there.

She decided to take Daniel at his word and shouted down
the hall, "You wouldn't happen to know where Fletcher keeps
the spare key to the filing cabinet back here, would you?"

The desk phone rang—it was Stacey. Charlotte must have
shouted louder than she intended if her voice had carried all the
way to the front desk. "It's one of the worst-kept secrets in the
entire office. He keeps the key behind your picture."

Key successfully located, Charlotte opened the cabinet and
began rummaging around for anything that might resemble

an employment document. Her husband was obviously not too concerned about easy document retrieval. If she had been working at his office full-time, the files would be stored in a more intuitive order. "I'm as bad as my mother," she announced out loud when she realized that she was criticizing his organizational methodology.

Due to the organizational system in the cabinet—or lack thereof—she couldn't be sure, but it almost appeared that at least one folder was missing as there seemed to be a gap from one section in particular. Charlotte was extremely familiar with the overall impact a stack of papers could make in relation to other folders, but eventually she found a selection of papers containing addresses and tax identification information, so she was reasonably sure she had found what she was seeking.

Charlotte was rather shocked by the sheer number of names and documents. She was also surprised to see how many names she didn't recognize at all and mentally chastised herself again for not paying more attention to what had been going on in Fletcher's work life over the last five years. Then she found Regan's file, and all thoughts of self-chastisement left her mind.

Here were multiple memos citing discussions between Fletcher and Regan on topics like consistent failure to show to work and unprofessional outbursts. Charlotte wasn't sure if Fletcher's working persona was the most patient man alive, if he either thought Regan could truly change her behavior if just placed in a supportive environment or if it was more an example of the naive optimism previously implied by Daniel. Charlotte tended to believe the latter. In either case, the evidence in front of her would have been enough to make anyone miserable in Fletcher's role.

Regan's periodic performance reviews were also in the folder. These showed that she had not been making idle boasts about her performance. Clearly, she met her numbers for appointments set and the conversion of those appointments to proposals, but the review also showed the percentage of time she had been out of the office. Fletcher may have thought he needed her, but to Charlotte's eyes, the cost of keeping her as long as he had really outweighed what she had brought in.

The next document was her tax identification forms. Charlotte snorted. The forms showed Regan's age to be in her late fifties. "A woman of that age is most certainly not going to change a lifetime of behavior because some guy in his midthirties wrote up some memos and created some pretty reports. Fletcher, you were just delaying the evitable, weren't you?" The document also included Regan's address.

After scribbling the addresses down, Charlotte once again stopped by Daniel's desk. "I think I would like to have a talk with Regan, after all, about her last few days and on the whole Marshall thing, but I am not familiar with the part of town her home is located in at all. Are you?"

Daniel took a look at the address and ran a quick map search. "That's what I thought. It's not the worst part of town, but it's not the best either. Are you planning on going there right now?"

"Well, I was. Are you saying I shouldn't?" Charlotte answered, her voice unsure.

"It's not that. You just probably don't want to get lost there after dark. You should be fine now though. If you would like, I can wrap up here and come with you so that you aren't going alone."

Charlotte thought about it. If Regan was still feeling hostile toward her husband, it might not be a terrible idea to have some additional strong-armed support. "Yes, I think that would helpful. Thanks."

"Not a problem. Meet you outside in fifteen?"

As Charlotte and Daniel pulled alongside the house matching the address from Regan's personnel file, Charlotte was immediately relieved that Daniel had offered to come along. What could have, at one point, been described as a lawn was dried out and dusty; the only showing of green was the ill-maintained box hedges in front of the building. The exterior paint color matched the brown of the dead grass. A short chain-length fence surrounded the parameter of the dwelling—the type that is better suited for keeping dangerous animals in than keeping dangerous individuals out. Other homes on the block were similar in appearance although this house looked slightly worse for wear than some of the others.

Charlotte opened the gate and went up the path toward the front door. As she got closer, she noted a spattering collection of assorted garden gnomes placed surrounding the box hedges—their faces dirty and paint mostly faded away. A stack of moldy old newspapers also littered the way.

Charlotte rang the bell, noting a bit of damage on the door and window frames, most likely caused by termites, while she waited for an answer. She mentally added yard and home maintenance to the list of things that she would now need to be responsible for. She hoped she would be able to find a way to prevent her own home from falling into similar disrepair, but wasn't even sure how to start their lawn mower nor did she know when she might have the energy to tackle it.

The door opened. The woman answering the door had thinning gray and blonde hair and a narrow face. Her skin had the premature lines and leathery texture of a person who had spent too long either smoking or in the sun or a combination of the two. She wore a scooped-top tee shirt—showing off the remnants of curves which had probably opened a number of doors during her youth, but just now served to reinforce the jarring boniness of her other edges—paired with highly cutoff jean shorts and strappy flip flops.

She smiled. "Yes?"

"Um, are you Regan Lordes?"

"For at least a few more months." Regan laughed, waving her bare fingers. The way she said this made Charlotte think that her response was a regular joke she told most people, one that obviously was hilarious to her. "And you are?"

"Oh yes, er, sorry. I'm Charlotte Row, um, er, Fletcher's wife?"

Regan's expression immediately changed, the jovial mood draining, replaced with icy resolve.

"What do you want?"

"Er, this is rather awkward . . ."

"Well then, maybe you shouldn't be here asking me about it."

"Ah, well, it's come to my attention that there was recently an incident at the office regarding an unhappy subcontractor and that the police were called. I was told that you were one of the witnesses and may have actually spoken to the individual. Is this true?"

"Of course it's true. It wasn't the first time either! Your husband is an absolute slime. Time after time, they would cry on my shoulder about how he had taken advantage of them. It just makes me sick to my stomach. I hope you've enjoyed spending all that money you've stolen from them!"

"I've not stolen a dime from anyone."

"Well, you might not have realized what was going on under your very nose. He did speak highly of you. He probably didn't want his princess to get her hands dirty, and he had to know that no decent person would want to continue to live with him if they knew what he truly was like."

"If this is true, why didn't you quit?"

"Who told you I didn't? Was it him?" Regan pointed at Daniel, just then noticing him. "Have you been spreading lies about me? I can't believe it! I thought you were my friend!" Regan's attention snapped back to Charlotte, not waiting for an answer, as if by "unfriending" Daniel had made him immediately cease to exist.

"I thought that Fletcher could be reasoned with, could be reformed. I tried so hard to protect those people. I knew that without me they would have no one at all to protect their rights. I've marched on the capital on multiple occasions! I know what it takes to keep greedy, selfish pigs like your husband from walking all over the little guy, but that day with Marshall was the last straw. After that, I knew Fletcher was never going to see how wrong his dealings were, and I left. You are here though, asking about Marshall, so I can only assume that you now realize how much I was saving that company. You're here to beg me to return, aren't you? Well, I won't. I am never setting another foot in the door of that building, especially not with that complacent bitch at the front desk. You can find some other way to make amends to Marshall and all of those other victims."

"Um, I still don't know what you are referring to exactly. You're saying that Fletcher wronged all of these people, but I just don't understand what he is supposed to have done. What did Marshall tell you? And do you think it was so bad that Marshall would retaliate physically in revenge?"

"Marshall wouldn't hurt a fly. He's a sweet man that just wants to better himself—live the American dream. He's new to the US, and when Fletcher gave him the big talk about his potential, he bought hook line and stinker. Of course he was upset when after the work was done, Fletcher refused to pay him. Any normal person would. Of course any decent person would never have placed someone else in that situation in the first place."

175

"What about his threats on Fletcher?"

"He's probably just watched a lot of US television and thought that he had to talk like that to get anywhere. He's not a rich man with the resources to sue for what he is owed. He's just barely a citizen—the law doesn't work for people like him. That's why I fight so hard."

"Listen, I can tell that you aren't my husband's biggest fan, but he's missing. I need to know if there is even a possibility that Marshall could have gone beyond verbal threats."

"If your husband is gone, then you should thank whoever did it for doing you a solid favor. You're much better off. He was only going to drag you down to his level."

"Well, I don't think so. I want to find him and bring him home."

"Then I guess I don't have anything more to say to you than what I have. If you still want to be with him, then you belong together and I want nothing more to do with you nor will I help you find him."

The door slammed close so fast and hard that it would have broken Charlotte's nose had she been standing a couple inches closer.

"For what it's worth, Charlotte, Fletcher wasn't running a scheme. We have a number of really excellent subcontractors who are really happy with us. Those that do the work like they are supposed to do quite well."

"Thanks, Daniel, and I mean it. I knew that she might still be angry with him when I came here, but I was not expecting that at all."

"Well, do you think you got what you needed?"

"I guess. It sounds like Marshall is probably just another dead end." Charlotte's shoulders dropped in defeat. "I guess I really have no choice but to find a way to keep living while the police do their job."

"And do you think you are going to be able to do that?"

"What, be able to wait on the police, or go on living?" Charlotte meant the statement to come across as slightly humorous, but no laughter managed to mix into her own. As they made their way toward Daniel's car, Charlotte's eyes lowered, and she took one last scan of her surroundings.

Out of the corner of her eye, she caught a splash of bright primary color wedged in between the bushes near the door. The color, so bold, felt completely wrong in the face of the bland building and dying grass, and Charlotte strained her eyes attempting to get a better view. The shape came into focus, a shape she knew so well—the shape of a child's shoe.

"Does Regan's daughter have any kids of her own?" A terrible, terrible hope began to take shape in Charlotte's heart; her pulse began to quicken.

"She might. I think she's mentioned being a grandma, but I'm not really sure. I don't know how often she sees him or her. Why?"

"She might be watching out of the window to make sure we leave, but I am sure that's a kid's shoe over there wedged under the bushes."

"That blob over there? How can you tell? It could be just one of those creepy looking gnomes."

"No, that's a shoe. I have located Jake's shoes in way too many random places all while doing five other things at the same time—such as while trying to get out of the door in under two minutes—not to be able to recognize a shoe when I see one, especially one that looks exactly like one of Jake's."

"Do you want to go back and ask her about it? Check shoe sizes, that sort of thing?"

"No, you heard her, she isn't willing to help. And if she has anything to do with their disappearance, I don't want to tip her off that we've noticed anything. Do you think you might be willing to move the car while I circle around back and see if I can see anything else lying around?"

"You want to sneak around?"

"Not sneak, investigate. Daniel, I have to do this one last thing. I'll sit back and wait by the phone for the police to call if I'm wrong, but I can't leave without at least looking."

Daniel must have seen a look of earnest desperation in Charlotte's eyes, as he said as he entered the car, "Well, if we are going to do this thing, you better get in. She needs to see us both leave." Charlotte hopped into the car and they cruised around the block, idling near the home that backed up to Regan's property.

Charlotte removed her heels as she exited the vehicle, mentally thanking herself for choosing to wear an outfit made up of mostly earth tones that allowed for a degree of flexibility.

It would not do to be caught with a wardrobe malfunction in addition to sneaking through private property. At least she wouldn't look like the stereotypical trespasser wearing all black and ski mask in summer. A combination of paranoia and panic fermented in the back of her mind. The resulting chemical imbalance produced a mental image she found hysterical, and Charlotte had to bite down on her tongue to keep from giving herself away with maniacal laughter.

"Thanks for not questioning me." Charlotte stated this with the assurance of a person who was going to do whatever it was they wanted to, regardless of whether or not the other person agreed with them, and was merely verbalizing the statement for appearance's sake. "I just need to take a quick glance around."

"Just don't get caught."

Charlotte hoped that the people who lived in the yard she was about to cross were off at work thus wouldn't notice a figure dressed in a business attire, on barefoot, creeping through their property and scaling the fence. If they did, she hoped that they didn't own a gun and weren't the type to shoot first and question later. She began to question her decision as she initiated her climb by shakingly grasping the fence, but then thought of Jake potentially being somewhere in that house at least at one time and steeled her resolve.

She passed her first hurdle without hearing anyone nearby sound an alarm and ran toward the back of Regan's house. The sickly box hedges continued around the base of the building, and Charlotte ducked in between them and under the few rear-facing windows to the best of her ability. A few branches and leaves affixed themselves to her hair, her feet protesting their unprotected state, and her arms were scratched as she inched closer to the base of the first window.

Once below the window, she listened for any sound of an occupant within. Not hearing a sound beyond the hum of the air conditioner, she decided to risk peeking in. As the lack of sound suggested, there was nothing there other than what must be Regan's bed and dresser. There was no evidence of a child recently in the room either.

Charlotte ducked back down and inched toward the second window. Once again, she waited a few moments before risking a glance up. This time, she was met with a curtained window. From her vantage point, she could see enough through the gauzy material to determine that the room she was spying on was a bathroom; once again, there was absolutely nothing to suggest that either Fletcher or Jake might have been there at one point.

A dog barked—a few houses away but closer than she would have liked—and Charlotte quickly retreated back down among the bushes. She attempted to still her racing heart as she heard the sounds of sirens in the distance. "Please let them be going somewhere else. Please!" she whispered to herself. Charlotte debated abandoning her plan as she could no longer be quite as certain as she was that the bright shape she had seen in the front of the house from a distance was a shoe. "Just one more window. I'll just look in one more." She began her approach. The dog barked again. Another dog, a closer one, answered back. Charlotte could feel her sweat pass over some of the scratches on her face and arms.

From within the house, she heard a muted curse shouting at the dogs to shut the hell up. The dogs responded by doubling up their efforts. A third entered into the conversation, most likely a beagle or beagle mix with a long drawn out howl. The voice from inside continued to shout obscenities at the noise. The sound of sirens continued to call in the distance. Charlotte's hearing was further crowded by the thumping of her heart in her ears. As all this noise began to crest, another sound emerged, one that silenced all of the others—the sound of a child crying. Not just any child. It was the sound she had heard a little over four years ago, and one that she would recognize until her faculties failed her.

Chapter 17

Women are like teabags. We don't know our true strength
until we are in hot water!

—Eleanor Roosevelt

Charlotte darted to the final window and carefully rose to peer into the room. Huddled small, frightened, and crying in the corner of the room furthest from the door was Jake. Her Jake. Alive. Separated from her only by a demented woman, some vinyl siding, and a few panes of glass. Charlotte looked at the ground immediately around her for something, anything that might break the glass but somehow not further damage her son. When nothing appeared to be readily available, she emerged from the bushes, and Valkyries would have taken pause meeting her.

She raced around to the front of the building, ringing the bell, banging on the door, and demanding admittance. Regan opened the door in self-righteous anger.

"Maybe I wasn't clear. Get off my—"

Charlotte silenced her with her fist. Charlotte had never been in a physical confrontation before, but that didn't stop her from dropping Regan to the ground with a single solid hit. She pushed the rest of the door open, barely breaking stride, as she stepped over Regan's limp form and raced deeper into the house. As it was an older home, the floor plan would not have been described as open. Dark faux wood paneling ran the length of the small foyer, and Charlotte found herself having to navigate through a narrow hallway as she attempted to locate the room which would have corresponded to the exterior window.

Only after she had forced her way into an empty room did enough of the initial adrenaline fade, causing her to momentarily regret not calling for the police or Daniel before barging her way and giving up her element of surprise. Even channeling the tiger mother as she was, Charlotte knew deep down that Regan was most likely merely stunned from her hit, and she still hadn't located Fletcher nor had seen any indication that he was also trapped within the house. Charlotte was momentarily afraid that her rash reaction at seeing her son may result in further harm to her husband. "He would have done the same," she thought, flinging open another door.

This time, she had chosen the correct door. Jake, who had cowered even further when the door opened, risked a glance up. His bright blue eyes ringed with red connected with her own, and all other thoughts and doubts in her fell away. He may have spoken aloud, but all she saw was a mouthing of the word "Mommy!" In an instant, she was at his side, cradling his body in her arms, both of them sobbing from joy. He felt lighter in her arms than she remembered, but she could not detect any surface wounds. Unfortunately, she had been so involved cataloging each and every detail of his form that she had completely forgotten about the inherent danger she had left lying at the front door until the door to the room slammed shut.

Charlotte, startled back to the present, swung her head toward the door, scooping Jake up in the process and only then noticing that the door lacked a doorknob. She could hear Regan cackling on the other side while they both listened to footsteps fading away. Unsure of what Regan intended to do to the both of them upon her return, and guessing that whatever it was would be unpleasant, Charlotte frantically looked around the room for something to pry the door open or otherwise help them escape.

The room itself did not contain much beyond a few faded plastic and wooden toys, some of which were identical to Jake's missing toys from his room at home. Regan must have grabbed these when she procured his summer clothes. Additionally, the room contained a small twin-sized bed with a flattened pillow and quilt, which had the aged appearance of a family heirloom but one that had not been particularly treasured.

Charlotte grabbed one of the toys, clenching it in her fist. She pushed Jake as far behind her as she could stand without losing complete physical contact. Covering her fist with a corner of the quilt, she slammed the toy through the window, shattering the glass. Some of the falling glass still managed to puncture both the fabric and her skin in the process. A few shards impaled themselves into her already damaged, unprotected feet. Charlotte did not notice. A part of her mind that was still functioning reveled in the fact that she just destroyed a fragment of Regan's family, although it was well short of making the two of them even.

Draping the windowsill with the quilt, she hoisted Jake over and gently lowered him into the bushes. A few more of the shards of glass scraped her side. She could tell that at least one of these shards had broken her skin as she felt the initial tension and then release of the slow flow of blood loss. "Run, Jake! Run past the fence and don't stop until you find someone to help us. I want you to use your outside voice and scream!"

"My outside voice?" Jake repeated uncertainly. "Aren't you coming, Mommy?"

"I'll be right behind you! Run, sweetie! Run!"

Jake turned and sprinted toward the fence. Charlotte just hoped that he would be able to scale the fence. Jake regularly climbed up playground equipment, but never at a ninety-degree angle and never under pressure. She also hoped that Daniel would still be close enough to take notice of him before anyone more sinister did.

She began her own escape. Charlotte was just positioning herself so that she would have maximum leverage of her body's weight with minimal additional damage when the door opened once again. Regan filled the opening with a gun in hand, pointed in her direction. "Leaving so soon? Don't tell me you changed your mind about wanting to be with Fletcher, especially after everything I just told him about you not giving up on him. He'll be crushed."

Charlotte glanced furtively back out of the window and was relieved to see that Jake was nearly to the fence; however, he was still in direct line of sight and would be an easy shot for Regan to take if she chose to harm them both. Regan may also not be bluffing about Fletcher also being located somewhere nearby. She had no choice but to follow Regan's commands. She had overpowered Regan once; she could only hope to do so again.

Chapter 18

Courage is fire, and bullying is smoke.

—Benjamin Disraeli

Regan grabbed Charlotte by the arm as she exited the room in a vice-like grip, painfully twisting Charlotte's limb in the process, to the point that Charlotte felt a tingle along its length. Charlotte began to doubt that overtaking this woman would be quite as easy as the first time. She felt Regan shove her down the hallway before yanking her to a halt outside one of the doors Charlotte hadn't previously tried while she had been so desperately searching for Jake.

"Watch your step. There are a few loose boards, and I would hate for you to get hurt." Regan smugly snorted as she opened the door to a stairway that could only lead to a basement. Regan hadn't exaggerated. The stairs creaked with every step, and she was further unbalanced when she discovered that the wooden railing was not firmly attached to any semblance of a solid surface beyond the first half of the staircase. Her body, with its injured sides, slammed into the stairway wall.

The second half of the staircase opened up to the poorly lit basement below. A few metal pillars broke up the space, supporting the floor above, and Charlotte could see a number of cobwebs and dust bunnies decorating the various nooks and crannies. Regan spoke up behind her, "Ah, Fletcher, your four o'clock arrived. Tsk tsk, you really shouldn't meet people looking like that. It's not professional at all." A garbled, moaning sound answered, hidden behind a metal shelving unit filed with a number of dusty Tupperware containers labeled with notes like "Xmas Decorations."

Regan pushed Charlotte toward the direction of the sound. There on the other side, hidden mostly in shadow, was Fletcher. As she stumbled closer, she could see that he was tied to a chair in the center of the space, the left side of his face nearly unrecognizable from bruises and scratch marks. His skin was pale and waxy, his eyes sunken. His lips were dried and chapped now, but the stains on his shirt and a few trails in between the grime made it clear that, at one point, there had been lines of drool before his internal moisture ran out. Fletcher made no motion that he recognized her nor attempted to open his eyes. Charlotte couldn't even tell if he realized she was there at all.

"What have you done to him?"

"His shouting was giving me a headache and was upsetting the boy, so I made him a little treat to help calm him down."

"You've drugged him!"

"Sure, hours ago. But don't you worry, he should be coming around soon enough to hear all about the poor choices you have made. All in all, I've been much more humane to him than he has been to all those innocents. I at least haven't taken away his chance for a better life. At least, I hadn't yet."

"How is this," Charlotte said, gesturing toward the incapacitated and bruised Fletcher as much as her limited mobility would allow, "a chance for a better life?"

"Well, you see, that's really not my fault at all." The darkness drew sinister shadows across Regan's face; however, her eyes flashed in fevered light.

"Not your fault? You kidnapped him and have been torturing him down here for a week." Charlotte reached for her husband only to be hauled back to Regan's side and full attention by a painful twist of her arm. Charlotte felt as if her arm might no longer be completely set in its socket.

"A small discomfort, but at least he knew that his son was better off and his wife had a real chance for happiness."

"What?"

"We may not have met, but he had told me enough to know that you were miserable. He would tell us all the time about how he had forgotten this or that for you or how Jake was making you crazy. I understand. Not everyone is cut out for being a parent, but I know that we women have to stick together, so I figured out a way that everyone could get what they deserved. I would raise Jake as my own and give him all the love and attention he needed. You would get to start over fresh to do whatever it is you do, and Fletcher would have a chance to repent and be redeemed. He never even saw it coming, that's how smug he was. But little old me brought the big man low, didn't I?" Regan slapped Fletcher. Charlotte started, instinctively trying to stop the motion. Regan yanked her by the hair, tearing some of the strands out from the scalp.

"And so the prideful is brought low. I made sure it looked like he had left you. You don't go through five husbands without knowing what that looks like. He should have left you if he was a decent human being! But you just couldn't accept it and move on, could you? You weak, hypocritical women make me so ashamed sometimes. You whine about how miserable your men make you, and yet do nothing about it. So you see, because you just couldn't stand to be an independent woman, it's your fault, not mine, that he's lost one of the last good things going for him"

Fletcher's head dropped forward, momentarily interrupting Regan's tirade. Regan checked her watch. "Oh, I can't have my new son running around at this time of night. That would be so irresponsible. You want to be with your husband so badly? Fine, here's your chance to reconnect." Regan pushed Charlotte forward and, as Charlotte attempted to regain her balance, raised the gun, quickly firing off shots into Charlotte's legs. She felt the bone shatter as she crumpled to the ground. "Now you two don't stay up too late!" Regan chuckled to herself before returning upstairs, leaving them in the darkness together.

Charlotte rapidly blinked her eyes, finding herself level with the floor. A few seconds passed before the pain in her legs could be processed by her brain. The scene in front of her briefly faded out to a blue light as her neurons finally made their unwelcome connections. She realized that she was screaming. The noises startled Fletcher back into semi-consciousness. Charlotte dragged herself over to Fletcher's side. She could feel small dirt particles rubbing against her damaged limb, and it was nearly enough to send her into oblivion.

"Char? Char? Is that you?" The sound of Fletcher's voice brought her back to the present.

"Fletcher," she whimpered, as she attempted unsuccessfully to inch closer, more dirt lodging itself into her wounds, "I'm here."

"Jake?"

"Jake is going to be safe." Her brain reached its saturation point with regards to pain management, and a blissful numbness began to spread throughout her body. "I know he is." Her voice began to break. "I got him out before she brought me down here. He has to have been able to climb the fence by now." In her mind's eye, she once again saw her little boy reaching the fence line, his pale thin legs, growing so much taller each day, pumping harder than she had ever seen. She was so proud of him. She hoped that by saying the words aloud, it would somehow make the action true. "Daniel knows I am here. He'll call for help. We are going to be okay."

"How long have I been down here?" Charlotte watched as Fletcher struggled against his bonds.

"A week."

"Oh god. Charlotte, I am so, so sorry!"

"What happened?"

"She's insane!"

"I've noticed." Charlotte began to forget why she was on the floor and why her husband was tied to a chair. Colors in her vision began to dull. "But how did she get you down here?" Why was he not helping her off the floor? She was beginning to struggle to make sense of her situation.

"Jake. She had Jake. I was packing our bags to go camping while he played outside and had to take a phone call. I looked up and he was gone! It was just a couple of minutes! Minutes! Then she called. She had been nearby, saw a child get injured though it wasn't serious, and recognized him as mine. She told me to come quick. When I got there, she stuck me with something. I sort of remember walking in here, but it's hazy. She told me that you were going to think I left with him. You never thought that I would do something like that, would you?"

Charlotte heard the words he was saying, but it took her a few moments to remember the events of the last few days. Her brain did not seem to be functioning quite as quickly as she might have liked. "I wanted not to believe it, but everything looked really convincing." It had looked that way, hadn't it? "My mom was convinced you'd gone, and I might as well not have bothered filing the report with the police."

"How could you think I would do something to you like that? I love you. You are my center. I wouldn't have had the guts to do any of this without you. You're a wonderful mom too. I would never keep you away from Jake. You have to know that."

"I kept thinking that maybe we've drifted so far apart over the last few months that you thought you'd be better off starting from scratch. I've looked at your reports in the office. I know how much stress you've been under."

"I'm so sorry I didn't tell you about everything going on at the office. I just really wanted to prove to everyone that I could do this, really make something. Yeah, it's not gone exactly according to plan, but we were really starting to get some major momentum in the last few weeks. It's actually been really exciting lately, but why would you say we've drifted apart?"

"You don't tell me anything anymore. I had to find out about the whole knife incident from Tom." Charlotte's voice started to slur, while Fletchers became more and more clear and coherent.

"Knife incident."

"So many? Regan's daughter."

"Oh no! That was definitely not a normal day. Is that how you knew to look here?"

"No. Fire truck. Freezer."

"Fire truck, freezer? What?" Charlotte did not immediately reply. "Charlotte? Charlotte! Oh my god, is that blood? She shot you? I thought I was dreaming still! What's that sound?"

Fletcher started to cough and gasp as he began to twist in the chair. Charlotte began to feel light-headed and a little chilled. She took a deep breath. The air smelled of campfire. Fletcher started rocking back and forth in his chair. Charlotte smiled and thought to herself, "What smart thinking, Fletcher brought a rocking chair along on this trip." She hadn't had a chance to really enjoy a camping trip with Fletcher in years. So nice of her mom to take care of Jake. And on such short notice too.

"Charlotte, hold on!"

Charlotte thought Fletcher was being quite silly. There was nothing around to hold on to, at least nothing for her to hold on to. He seemed to be still attached to the chair as it fell over onto its side. He began to wiggle and squirm in order to get closer to her. She didn't know exactly why he didn't just walk over to her, but she would be glad when he reached her. The night was really beginning to get chilly. Charlotte wondered where all the stars were tonight. No sooner had she thought this than she started to see lazy fireflies fluttering down around them—an entire swarm of fireflies. A few bit her. She half-heartedly waved it away. Everything grew a little darker.

"Baby! I love you! I don't tell you that enough, but I need you! Stay with me!"

Charlotte thought back to one of their family's last camping trips. Fletcher had been showing Jake how to build a campfire.

"Now you see, Jake, this is what we call an ember." Jake had stood slightly back from his father in rapt attention. "This little glow will make or break a fire. Too much air and it will blow out. Smother it and it will choke, and your fire will go out. But here's the really important thing, Jake. As long as you keep this little flame going, you can rebuild your fire nearly from scratch, which can save you a lot of time and help you build a better, stronger fire. But if you are completely done, you have to extinguish it altogether or it can become a really dangerous thing."

A brightness like an angry sun filled her vision, silhouetting Fletcher, still lying on his side but nearer to her. She felt the heat radiating from it, and yet was icy cold. The brightness became unbearable, and she closed her eyes against it. She vaguely heard Fletcher gasping and sobbing and saying her name, but he sounded miles away. Charlotte found that for the first time, in what felt like years, she no longer had tears to shed.

"I'm so, so sorry, Char."

The angry red light shining through her eyelids began to fade.

"Stay with me."

Something unpleasant latched onto the surface of her face. She didn't have the energy to attempt to pull it away.

"Just a little longer."

She was jostled around. She had no idea what was going on, but whatever was causing the commotion was really cutting into her rest.

"Got you."

The words made Charlotte think of Regan's gloating smile, and she began to feel her heart race once more in a panic.

"Easy, easy, take a deep breath."

She felt a pinch along her arm. Why could Fletcher not allow her to get some sleep? She opened her eyes. Giant yellow and black bees were all around her, and she seemed to be on a surfboard of some kind. She closed her eyes and stilled her body as much as possible.

"I've got a response!"

She floated, filled with boundless joy. Nothing would be able to reach her so high up. She decided to risk another look around. The bees were gone. Instead she watched one of Jake's firemen videos play out. She was going to have a talk with him about turning the volume up too high. The entire neighborhood probably could hear it from here. She closed her eyes again.

The next time she opened her eyes, she realized that she was outside on the street. A number of cars were nearby. She was still floating, moving closer to the flashing lights. One of the flashing lights illuminated Jake, who had been rapturously watching the scene before him while standing beside a very tall man she vaguely recognized. She saw him take notice of her. Jake started to run toward her, but the man grabbed hold of him, keeping him back from her.

"No! No! Not again!" Charlotte began to writhe around, only then realizing that she was restrained. "You can't have him!"

"Don't struggle. He's fine!"

Charlotte instantly hated whoever that voice belonged to.

"I'm going to need some help here."

Charlotte was pinched again and everything faded to black.

Chapter 19

I believe that everything happens for a reason. People change so that you can learn to let go, things go wrong so that you appreciate them when they're right, you believe lies so you eventually learn to trust no one but yourself, and sometimes good things fall apart so better things can fall together.

—Marilyn Monroe

Charlotte awoke in a hospital bed, her leg restricted within a cast and her arm sore from an IV connection. The curtain surrounding her bed moved, allowing Fletcher to enter into the enclosed area.

"Hi, beautiful, glad to see you back with us."

"You're not going to win any pageants right now yourself, you know." Fletcher wasn't either. The bruises on his face had faded to a rosy purplish color, and a few of the deeper cuts were held together by adhesive bandages.

"Maybe not, but chicks dig scars." Fletcher smiled as he sat down in the small chair located near the side of the bed.

"Is that a fact?"

Fletcher reached over to caress her hand, and Charlotte felt a slight pain causing her to shudder.

"Oh! Sorry, baby, I didn't mean to hurt you."

"I'll be okay, right?"

"You should be. You were strong enough to beat the shock, blood loss, and smoke inhalation. I think you will be able to recover from a broken bone."

"Oh, that's all? Where's Jake?"

"Getting spoiled by your mother and your sister, where else? Unfortunately, Regan must have double backed to our house for most of his clothes after I was out of commission, so they are ensuring he has a brand new wardrobe. Of course, he is insisting on brand-new fire truck pajamas." The smile faded from Fletcher's face, the joking mode evaporating. "Charlotte, I don't know that she is going to forgive me anytime soon. Even if I hadn't put you in danger, she told me what it looked like. At length. In only slightly varying degrees of hysteria. About the car at the bus station, the bags, everything. If our situation had been reversed, I don't know that I would have continued to believe that what everyone else was telling me was wrong. How did you know that I hadn't left?"

"I saw your message?"

"My message?"

"Yeah. You know, how you left the fire truck in the freezer, telling me that something was wrong and that you'd gone for Jake."

"What fire truck? Our freezer?"

"You know, Jake's small fire truck. The one we gave him last Christmas. Mom found it in our freezer."

"And you thought this was a message from me?"

"Yeah, we had agreed on the whole code after that last sci-fi movie. The one about smoke signals?"

"Charlotte, I didn't leave a message."

"Of course you did. When I saw that, I just knew that something was wrong."

"No, Charlotte. I didn't. You've complained a hundred times that I am terrible about telling you where I am going. I didn't even think to leave a note. I wanted to take a Coke with me on the trip, but we didn't have any cold ones. I must have grabbed the truck and put it in the freezer rather than a can. I really wasn't paying attention."

There was a long pause while neither spoke for several minutes. Charlotte watched numbers change on the monitor next to her. Fletcher, looking at his hands, quietly spoke again, "I haven't been paying attention to a lot besides work. I see that now. I really do want us to be partners. I do. I just . . ."

Charlotte didn't dare speak. She was afraid that any sudden movement would startle him back into silence.

"I just haven't been around . . . I haven't been there for you and Jake."

Charlotte sighed. "Honestly, I've learned that I haven't exactly been around for you either. I can't help thinking that I might have been able to locate you both sooner if only I had done a better job of asking you what was going on."

"I'm not sure I would have told you even if you had asked. I was relieved you stopped asking for the details. I just know how trapped you must feel, stuck in a job you don't like just so we have a security net. I didn't want to burden you further with complaints about my job, especially as you would think that by being the owner, I would be able to make more of a difference. No one ever tells you about the little things that keep cropping up and positively drain you. I wanted to prove to the world that I could be successful on my own. I didn't want someone to think that I was just some slob, mooching off my wife. The thing about it is that it always looks like the next month is going to be the one when it all changes. I mean, you should see some of the contracts that come across my desk, but it was like whenever something good would happen, someone or something would come up that I would be forced to deal with."

"I think I know what you mean. Daniel told me about some big contract with Avnex coming in, but I also got a call from a patent troll about a potential lawsuit."

"Daniel thinks he has landed Avnex? Oh, that's fantastic news! Wait, how do you know that? And what do you mean a lawyer called you?"

"I've been filling in for you this past week at the office. About the lawyer, there's probably a cease-and-desist letter in the mailbox by now. He claims that you are knowingly infringing on a client's intellectual property and claims to have some documents from the office to support his claim. At first, I was just there to try to see if I could find a clue as to where you might be. It also gave me an excuse to get out of the house. I kept seeing Jake everywhere and couldn't handle thinking I'd never see him again. Then after the fire truck, I told myself that if I could keep it alive, I could somehow keep you both alive as well."

"You are amazing. I've not told you that for a long, long time, but you are. You could have let it all crumble, and no one would have thought badly of you for doing so at all. I don't know if I could have done it, but I know now that I would not be here at all if it wasn't for you."

He leaned over her, brushing a few errant strands of hair out of her face, and ever so gently, as if the slightest weight could further injure her, placed a kiss on her forehead.

"No more secrets or lies by omission. This time, I promise, we will be partners in truth, and if the business crashes, so be it."

Extremely regretful to ruin the mood, but finding herself with no choice after Fletcher's speech, Charlotte told him about the call with Peter Demsey and the offer on the business. At first, Fletcher appeared to be intrigued by the prospect of a buyer; but as Charlotte explained the rest of the conversation, including the lowball offer and Peter Demsey's insensitivity, Fletcher's features became sharp and serious.

Fletcher brought out his cell phone.

"Um, I don't think you are supposed to have phones in here," mentioned Charlotte, extremely regretful now that she had said anything at all. She had rather enjoyed the undivided attention of her husband.

"This won't take but a minute.

"Peter, this is Fletcher.

"Yes, I'm back.

"Charlotte told me about your lead on a buyer. You can let them know we're not selling.

"Oh, and, Peter?

"You're fired."

Fletcher ended the call and buried the phone deep, deep in his pockets.

"Well, I guess I am going to have to find new representation."

Charlotte laughed. "I may know a guy. I just have to check out my LinkedIn connections."

"Well, aren't you just the corporate titan. I am curious to know what other skills you acquired while I was gone. Enough about work. What I care about now is how long it is going to be before you are back on your feet so that I can convince you to get back off them." Fletcher smiled his secret sexy smile, sending Charlotte's heart and hormones racing. She was partially afraid that the sensors and probes connecting her to the beeping machine would give her mood away to the nursing staff. As she gazed back hungrily upon him, she realized she didn't care. She was in love with, and wanted, the man standing beside her, and she was not ashamed to admit it.

The following day, Charlotte was released from the hospital. As she would be unable to navigate around her home, let alone the rest of town for the next few weeks, her mother had volunteered to continue to stay at their home in order to help out with the chores and Jake. Jake was overjoyed with this arrangement as his experience with Regan had made him extremely reluctant to leave the side of his family members. Charlotte didn't blame him. She was equally reluctant for him to be out of her sight, and the narrow gap that her mother allowed between herself and either Charlotte or Jake never exceeded more than a yard.

She and her mother had both been in the den, staring at Jake play as if he might vanish if they so much as blinked while Fletcher examined what food items remained in the fridge and pantry, when the doorbell rang. Her mother opened the door, allowing a pair of police officers to enter into the room. Jake dropped his toy and ran over to his mother, clutching her hand.

"I apologize for not standing up," Charlotte said to the officers while gesturing for them to have a seat while Fletcher entered from the kitchen to sit next to his wife.

Her mother took Jake by his other hand, leading him away. "I know, Jake, let's build a fort in your room!"

"First off, let me say how relieved all of us on the force are to see you, Mr. Row, and your son back at home and you, Mrs. Row, recovering."

Charlotte chose not to make a witty retort, but it was a choice that took a lot of effort to make.

"We came here today to also give you an update on our own investigation. When you came to the station last Mrs. Row, you had asked us to investigate a Marshall Thomas in connection with Fletcher's disappearance. We did follow up with this lead and tracked him to his apartment. While there is no evidence to suggest that Mr. Thomas was in any way connected to Mr. Row's disappearance, when questioned, he did admit to have been working with a Mrs. Regan Lordes on what could be considered corporate espionage. Regarding the espionage, he claims that Mrs. Lordes approached him with documents obtained from a locked filing cabinet within Mr. Row's office and that she had asked him to deliver those documents to a specific address. We looked up that address and found it to be the location of Davidian LLC, which we believe is a competitor of yours. Is that correct?" Fletcher nodded in confirmation.

The police officer continued, "Mr. Thomas went on to say that he did this because Mrs. Lordes claimed that Davidian would pay a portion of settlement funds to the person who delivered the documents to them. When we approached Davidian, a representative denied any involvement to such an arrangement, as you might expect; but I guess Mr. Thomas was just desperate enough to believe her. He is being charged, and you'll be notified of any court dates related to the office theft. You may also be interested to learn that when further pressed, Mr. Thomas went on to admit that he has been routinely involved in a number of shakedown scams targeting startup businesses. He poses as a potential customer or vendor and then threatens the owner with a series of negative reviews unless the owner agrees to pay him some form of compensation. If the owner refuses to make a payment, he retaliates by waging a negative social media campaign or reporting the owner to an organization, like the better business bureau. It seems that when you weren't in the office that day but Regan was, he chose to abandon his standard con for one that seemed, at least to him, as having a greater chance for success."

Charlotte asked the question that had been on her mind since the initial euphoria of being reunited with her family had faded. "What about Regan? What are you going to do about her?"

"Well, unfortunately, that news isn't as promising. Our reports state that Mr. Row's associate, a Mr. Daniel Wallace, was located behind the property when the events occurred. He states that he saw a young boy matching the description of your son running away from the property and did not immediately return as the boy was quite hysterical and understandably unwilling to get into a car with a stranger. When he did arrive back at the scene, the fire was already in process, but there was no sign of Mrs. Lordes. We were not even notified that Mr. Row had been found until after the blaze was contained and, until then, had no reason to suspect that Mrs. Lordes might be involved in the abduction as well as the theft. We did revisit the bus station and can confirm that Mrs. Lordes was the only person in your vehicle and must have taken a city bus from the hub back home after depositing your car in the long-term parking lot. She went to a lot of effort to make it seem like you had left on your own."

"So you are telling us that not only has she gotten away and could return at any time to harm my family, she's a master criminal too!" Fletcher nearly shouted, the remaining scrapes and bandages on his face becoming more visible as his complexion became reddened. "What are you going to do to ensure our safety? What are you going to do to catch that maniac! I hope you are willing to do more than you did to locate our son!"

"Sir, we understand your concern and we are taking this matter very seriously. We've notified the police in Florida, where her daughter resides, to be on the lookout if she makes contact. They've acknowledged the request, but have not yet interviewed Ms. Lordes's daughter. In the meantime, we will be assigning a patrol to watch your property to ensure that she takes no further retaliation.

Charlotte chose to diffuse the rapidly intensifying situation by thanking the officers for the update while asking them to continue to keep them abreast of any progress they made tracking Regan down. Meanwhile, Fletcher continued to make sure everyone knew how confident he was that the police officer's plan would be an effective safety measure. He was firing up the computer, muttering about looking up self-defense and basic weapons safety classes before the officers had pulled out of the driveway.

The explanation that the policemen had offered as to Marshall's complaints and appearance at the office did make a lot of sense to Charlotte, but Regan had referred to Fletcher as a fraud so often that she decided that she at least needed to air the question. As soon as Fletcher had returned from shutting the door behind the departing policemen, Charlotte asked, "You wouldn't have known that Marshall was running a con. Have you ever not paid people because Archer Service Solutions was so far in the red and failure to complete the work was a convenient excuse?"

"Yes, there have been months where the account dipped below the line, and yes, I've had to pull money from our personal account as a loan to cover the business for a couple of days. And I'm sorry that I never told you about that, I should have cleared it with you. I only did that to ensure that all of our employees and vendors were paid on time. I have never once cheated anyone out of money they truly earned. Marshall's work was truly awful. I have plenty of documentation back at the office that clearly shows he was not meeting the terms of our agreement."

"I also found out that you've been paying yourself more for the last few months and putting the difference into a secret bank account. Why would you hide something like that from me?"

"Oh. You found that."

"Yes. That."

"Well, that's a different sort of surprise."

"I'm listening."

"It might be better if I showed you something." Fletcher escaped Charlotte's probing glare and went back out into the garage. A few minutes later, he reemerged holding a stack of papers. Charlotte released the breath she had been holding, not realizing until that moment that even after what they had been through, there was still a nugget of doubt buried deep within her that wouldn't have been terribly surprised to hear the sound of the engine roar and rubber squeal.

He brought the papers over to her and fanned them out so that she could better see.

"Honey, I truly, truly had no idea you felt that we were so far apart. Just another thing I hadn't paid attention to. The reason I had the separate account set up was that I have been saving month by month as much as I thought I could manage to pay for a trip for us. All of us. I've been putting the money away so that I wouldn't be tempted to spend it on the business and have been making payments toward the various travel agency and tour groups."

Charlotte didn't know what to say. Before her were documents showcasing one of the dream trips they had always talked about but never thought they could afford. There was even an itinerary for her mother. "So do you think she might finally find it in her heart to forgive me by then?"

"I don't know. It does look like you've already ruined the trip for her."

"What do you mean?" Fletcher asked, shocked and slightly disappointed

"Well, it looks like you've already organized everything. What is she going to do with herself?"

Fletcher's shoulders relaxed, realizing Charlotte was only joking. "Well, I guess I can turn her loose on the agent now that the surprise has been ruined."

Charlotte threw her head back in laughter. "We'll have a whole new trip. She'll surprise us both!"

Fletcher leaned in, clasping Charlotte's hand in his. "Whatever makes her happy. I don't care where we go or what we do as long as you are with me. I want you with me always. I love you."

Epilogue

It may be hard for an egg to turn into a bird: it would be a jolly sight harder for it to learn to fly while remaining an egg. We are like eggs at present. And you cannot go on indefinitely being just an ordinary, decent egg. We must be hatched or go bad.

—C. S. Lewis

As Charlotte stepped out of Whitman and Starns for the last time, the sun momentarily blinded her as it reflected off the glass protecting her family pictures contained within her box of possessions. She stood for a moment to rest before trekking out the rest of the way to her car, her leg, though long since freed from the cast, still weaker than she would have liked. She thought of their upcoming trip and was glad that they had made sure that there was transportation and porter service included everywhere they were going.

She opened the trunk of her car and began reshuffling the stored paintings so that nothing would get damaged in transit between her office and her new studio. She still could not believe that Rhea had been stockpiling her work all this time for a potential gallery showing through one of her family connections, and she was even more shocked to hear that Rhea had arranged not only a sale of many of the existing pieces but also a commission for another show. Charlotte had begged Rhea to accept a portion of the proceeds as way of thank you, which she had refused, but had accepted to work out a more formal representative agreement for pieces created after Charlotte and Fletcher returned from their trip.

The money had been just enough to get her car tuned up and to pay the deposit toward a shared studio's rent. Rhea's unexpected work was also allowing her the freedom and flexibility to reduce the number of hours that Jake spent at the day care center. Things might still be tight financially for at least the next few months, especially after their upcoming vacation, but Charlotte felt more at ease about their situation. Both she and Fletcher were pursuing their dreams, and any sacrifices they made were made jointly and with eyes wide open.

Charlotte woke her phone and dialed Fletcher to give him an update of her last day.

"So does this mean you are a free woman now?"

"Yep."

"How did they send you off?"

"Apparently, Richard didn't tell Whitman that I was leaving the firm until about ten this morning. He never thought I was serious and kept waiting for me to change my mind. He didn't want Whitman to know that I was exercising, and I quote, 'bad judgment,' which would further diminish my reputation at the firm especially after my recent absence."

"What did Whitman say when he found out?"

"Well, I don't know what he said to Richard as that was behind a closed door, but I do know that Richard is going to be enjoying some time off himself. Right before I left, Whitman came over to tell me that there would be a spot for me if this didn't work out and offered to help you out with the response to any other troll that thinks of you and an easy target on the house. You are absolutely sure you can pick up our insurance?"

"Paperwork is signed, sealed, and delivered. Are you having second thoughts?"

"I am scared, but really, really excited."

"I can relate, but I am sure we can find a larger spot for you over here too if you get bored. I am still amazed you were able to pull that whole Avnex proposal together on the fly like that."

"Thanks. I'll be right by later on to look over some of those other files after I get everything set up at the studio. How's my mom working out?"

"You know, I was really on the fence about having your mom in my office, but she's got us running like a machine now. She's also taken over marketing distribution. I've seen our name everywhere!"

"I can believe it. So you think it is going to work out with her over there?"

"I wasn't sure about how well it would work out when you first suggested it. I mean, she was really quick to think the worst of me."

"Yeah, but you said yourself that the evidence wasn't exactly helping you."

"I know, I know, and if having a watch from time to time helps to remind me to stay focused, I can live with it, especially if she keeps up like she has been."

"How about Stacey, how's she doing?"

"That kid of hers must have really given her some experience on the tough sell. She's taken to inside sales like she was born for it. She's actually set up more than double Regan's best day of solid leads."

"And her kid, any more problems?"

"Daniel actually has started to do a Big Brother program sort of thing with him. It seems to really be helping. She hasn't had any family emergencies lately. Oh, speaking of Daniel, you would not believe what he told me today."

"I'm listening."

"He was called about a job reference."

"Oh." Charlotte wasn't quite sure where Fletcher was going with this. While someone calling Daniel as a reference could be somewhat unexpected given his background, she failed to see how it was exactly noteworthy.

"The person on the other line was asking Daniel to be a reference for Regan."

Charlotte gasped. "Oh my god, are you serious? What did he tell them?"

"What do you think he told them? He told them the truth and got their address. I've already sent the lead to the police, not that I expect them to do much with it. At least we know she's out of state, at least for now, and not just sitting down the street waiting for us to stop paying attention."

"That's really, really great news. But wow, if I didn't know exactly how delusional she could be, I would never have believed she would put you guys down on her resume. There are no words to describe that psycho. But enough about her. I don't want to ruin what is shaping up to be a great day. Do you think you are going to be home for dinner tonight? Your calendar showed you have a meeting with Avnex later."

"I do, but Daniel has everything running smoothly with them." Daniel was turning out to be a stupendous find for Fletcher. He was loyal and seemed to be as enthusiastic and dedicated to the company as Fletcher. Fletcher was already beginning to transition some of his work onto Daniel's eager shoulders.

"I should be home on time. Do you want me to pick up Jake? We can go play some basketball so that you can head out with the ladies."

"That's okay, I think I'd like to spend some time with my guys. How about I join you for a game of horse? My leg could use a little exercise." She stretched out her leg and felt a slight protest of pain as if on cue. "You wouldn't mind me sweating a little with you?"

Fletcher's voice took on a slightly husky humor. "I can think of a few other exercises we can do afterward too. It's always best to make sure to stretch following a workout."

Although her comment had been made innocently, Charlotte's mind immediately picked up on Fletcher's innuendo, adjusting her own tone accordingly. "I think I might be able to manage that. It's a date."

Charlotte smiled to herself as she hung up the phone, her car starting the first time and purring in its good working order. The police may have not been able to successfully nail down Regan's location, but Daniel's call today should at least reboot the search effort. Enough time, however, had passed for the police to begin scaling back their surveillance efforts, and Charlotte's heart rate was no longer set racing whenever she caught the slightest whiff of smoke in the air, which was a good thing considering her cooking. As she drove away, all the lights ahead of her were green, and the future was looking bright.

About the Author

Allie Potts, born in Rochester, Minnesota, sometime between Generation X and Generation Y, was moved to North Carolina at a very early age by parents eager to escape to a more forgiving climate. She has since continued to call North Carolina home, settling in Raleigh in 1998, halfway between the mountains and the sea. She and her husband of ten years, both graduates of North Carolina State University and parents of two small boys, took on the risk of launching a small business before the height of the Great Recession, an experience that continues to be both rewarding and terrifying.